a death
twice avenged

a death twice avenged

Another Case for Inspector Wickfield

Julius Falconer

PNEUMA SPRINGS PUBLISHING UK

First Published in 2009 by:
Pneuma Springs Publishing

A Death Twice Avenged
Copyright © 2009   Julius Falconer
ISBN: 978-1-905809-61-5

Pneuma Springs Publishing

A Subsidiary of Pneuma Springs Ltd.

7 Groveherst Road, Dartford Kent, DA1 5JD.

E: admin@pneumasprings.co.uk

W: www.pneumasprings.co.uk

A catalogue record for this book is available from the British Library.

To
Jules and Donald Macmillan
in gratitude

Julius Falconer

One

*T*his is a story of murder. It is also a story of revenge. It tells of human weakness, deception and fallibility, of poor judgement and of wickedness; but its message – although it has not got one - is far from being straightforward condemnation. Its heroine – although she is not heroic – tries to avenge her father's death because she sees no satisfactory alternative: there is no one else to do it. The question that this raises is whether her assessment is correct - or fatally flawed. In that sense, this tale is a parable: it asks author and readers where their judgement lies but does not itself propose an answer. The question is important: is evil punished? If so, by whom? and when? and, we must add also, how?

Prefaces are rather tedious, to some people's way of thinking. Scott's lengthy dissertations before he begins his novels, addressed to Dr Dryasdust or to Jedediah Cleishbotham, are prosy and irrelevant: let the novel begin! (Prosy and irrelevant like the novels themselves, I hear you say. No, no, that cannot be allowed to pass. Scott's novels are an endless source of information and entertainment, many of them jostling for place in the top ranks of English literature – in my opinion). That is why these opening remarks are cunningly passed off as the book's first chapter rather than as a preface; but of course the impatient reader is welcome to proceed speedily to chapter two, in which the first murder, which so to speak sets the ball rolling, is recounted! The reader who does so, however, will miss, ahem, important insights into the workings of Detective Inspector Wickfield's mind.

On the question of revenge, the reader is likely to take one of three stances. The first stance is that, since there is no final tribunal in which right and wrong are judged, human justice must detect and punish as best it may. Humanity has devised many systems of justice, some less satisfactory than others, and it is rationally possible to hold that the perfect system has yet to be devised, but that, however inadequate, a system of justice worked on essentially rational lines is better than no system at all. It might be considered that this attitude labours under two major flaws. It is patently clear that many crimes remain undetected and unpunished: this seems rather a pity; and human justice is such that sometimes the guilty go free while the innocent are condemned (which, while being preferable to its contrary, is still very unsatisfactory). The second stance is that, formal forensic justice being so unsatisfactory, *vide supra*, the individual – or the clan – must himself or itself shoulder the responsibility of punishment. This justifies feuds and vendettas, reprisals and what the text-books are pleased to call occult compensation (which some casuists justify). This attitude might be thought to promote a system of retribution with the potential to spiral out of control, to perpetuate itself; and furthermore, there is no guarantee of justice, since the only justice practised is that set by the perpetrators. The third stance is likely to be adopted by religious believers the world over: only the Supreme Being – Brahman, Jahweh, God, Allah, The Name – can fairly administer justice. For example, the Jewish and Christian Bibles contain many injunctions to the effect that revenge can safely, and must, be left to God: justice is his prerogative. The Book of Proverbs solemnly intones: 'Do not say, "I shall pay you back for this wrong". Wait rather for the Lord!' The drawback of this approach is that it requires a considerable level of faith in an afterlife, and many people of otherwise unimpeachable wisdom and learning lack it.

It will probably become apparent that the hero of this novel, Detective Inspector Stanley Wickfield, seeks to combine the first and third hypotheses outlined above. He is a product of his age, naturally, but he is endowed with enough education and intelligence to rise above narrow considerations of particular fact and to embrace wider issues of principle. He was born in 1921 into a middle-class family in the Midlands of England. His police career proceeded according to established pattern. He married, had two sons (neither of whom entered the police force). Successes came his way, achieved through a combination of perseverance, open-mindedness and intuition. He was popular with his peers and with his inferiors, because with him there was no side. He made mistakes, and the present narrative contains a gross example that nearly costs him the case. Above all, however, he is a thinking man, with an eye permanently trained on the cosmos.

He had given the matter of retribution some considerable thought. He was a believer, a practising Christian, and he therefore accepted biblical teaching as normative – if one could only find it in the many lengthy and contradictory documents contained in the Bible. When scholarly Christians disagreed amongst themselves, what hope was there for the layman? He accepted the general principle that God is the ultimate and sole, truly just avenger. Retribution takes place beyond death, after a scrupulous trial in which individuals are invited to give an account of their life and to advance any argument they choose to justify their acts, words and thoughts. However, if society left revenge entirely to God, human systems of fairness and balance collapsed: the law of the jungle prevailed, and Wickfield could not justify that on his understanding of human life and society. He therefore worked hard to bring criminals to justice, if only to get them off the streets and save further sufferers from falling victim to their wiles. In this he liked to think that he was at one with all his colleagues in the police force. The punishment of offenders was not, he thanked divine goodness, his responsibility, as that was a more complex and an altogether harder undertaking.

In this present account of a case that occupied him off and on for some months in the years 1970 and 1971, while he sympathised with the girl, he could not help feeling that there was an alternative to her strategy and that it would have saved a great deal of unhappiness. And so to our tale.

Imagine a substantial, detached house on the edge of an attractive Midlands town. It is the residence of a widowed businessman and his only daughter, a girl of five. Although his commercial premises – factory and offices - are in Worcester, the owner has chosen to live in the smaller town of Evesham (variously pronounced, as locals will tell you, Eve-shum, Ever-shum or Asum, and known affectionately to many as The Sham). The front-door leads into a spacious hall, with doors off to right, to left and ahead, and a flight of white-painted, carpeted stairs leading to the upper floor. The right-hand door leads into a sitting-room with a large bay-window at the front of the house, the left-hand door to a little-used dining-room. The two other doors lead respectively to a snug and the kitchen, both of which in turn give access to the garden. It is late evening, and the suburban world is dark except for the wan light shed by street-lamps. The owner of the house is entertaining a visitor in the sitting-room. His daughter has been in bed for several hours. It should be a typical scene of middle England: calm, civilised, time-hallowed; but it is not.

Two

The little girl sitting on the stairs in her night-clothes heard the voices raised in anger. The shouting had woken her, and she had crept out of bed, frightened and uncertain. She dared not descend the staircase but sat trembling at the top, unable to return to bed. She could see light streaming through the living-room door into the hall, and the familiar furniture – the hall-stand, a telephone-stool, a wooden settle containing the croquet set - reassured her that this was not a nightmare; and she recognised her father's voice.

'Don't be ridiculous,' she heard her father saying. 'Have some sense, man, before you say something stupid. I'm not going in with you, and that's final. I can't afford it, for a start, and I think your scheme's risky. You can play for high stakes, if you like, but I've got a kid to consider, and I'm not going to put my hard-earned money where I might lose the lot.'

'Are you saying I'd make a poor associate?' she heard a man's voice raised in reply, 'because if you are, you'd better be careful. I'll have you know I'm a far cleverer operator than you'll ever be, and if you don't recognise a unique opportunity when you see it, you're a bigger mug than I took you for. I tell you it'll work: money, financial and commercial success, lucrative deals at home and abroad. All I need is a little cash, enough to flesh out the figures, and you're a fool not to go in with me.'

The little girl listened as the conversation continued, afraid to advance, afraid to retreat.

'If it's such a clever scheme, go to a bank!'

'You know damn well I can't do that, not since I went bankrupt.

Banks won't look at me, but you've got the necessary capital. All you lack is a bit of savvy and a spirit of adventure. Come on, Len, what do you say?'

'No, no, and again no! I'm not to be bullied into any scheme, Hick, and I'd be glad if you'd take your hare-brained plans elsewhere else and leave me in peace. When will you understand that I'm just not interested?'

'You're turning up the chance of a life-time. And what's more, you're preventing me from making a lot of money. This is the chance I've been waiting for, and you're the only thing in my way.'

'I'm not in your way, not in the least. You go ahead, but it'll have to be without me.'

'Damn you, Len, damn you to hell. You're the only hope I've got. After all these years, don't you owe me anything?'

'I owe you friendship, Hick, but that doesn't mean putting my family at risk. Look, we've talked enough. You'd better go before we fall out.'

'Len, I must have that money. I'm in debt again. I'm ruined if I can't make a lot of money, and fast. You've got to help me. I shall use force'.

'I haven't got to help you at all. I can give you a loan, but the amount you want is beyond me, and in any case I'm not risking it. Now please go away, and let's hear no more about it.'

The little girl heard a vicious snarl of anger and sounds of a scuffle. Rooted to the spot, she shook with fright. The furniture in the living-room crashed here and there. Vases fell to the ground amidst the sounds of shattering glass. She heard panting and thuds. Then suddenly there was silence. After a short time, the living-room door was jerked from within, and a man in an overcoat hurried into the hall, wrenched the front-door open and disappeared into the night, slamming the door shut behind him.

Rachel was, inevitably, a hopeless witness. She could remember nothing of the conversation. The only item of information that could in any way be considered useful was the stranger's name: Mick. Her conversation with the police-woman was almost completely unenlightening, beyond the basic item that she had heard part of the conversation as she sat on the stairs.

'Rachel, pet, there's nothing to be frightened of now. You're safe with us. I want you to tell me all you can remember about last night. Take your time. Cuddle up to your Auntie Sarah and think hard. Do you know what time in the evening it was when you first heard voices downstairs? Had you been in bed long, or only just gone up?'

Rachel shook her head.

'You obviously recognised your dad's voice. Did you recognise the other voice at all?'

Rachel shook her head.

'Had you ever heard it before?'

Another shake of the head.

'Can you describe the man you saw leaving the house? Anything about him? Was he wearing a coat, for example? Was he tall? Young? Can you remember anything that was said?'

None of these questions, so important to the police inquiry, was met with anything but a denial, a mute shake of the head, as the eyes stared out uncomprehendingly. The aunt, summoned in haste by the char-lady on her discovery of the murder-scene that morning, had succeeded in extracting from the traumatised child the name of the stranger. Otherwise the police inquiry was starting from a *tabula rasa*.

*L*eonard and Miriam Appleton lived in a detached house on the edge of the town. A short drive, winding through a shrubbery, led to a 1930s double-fronted property typical of its age. Neat gardens girdled it, tended by an assiduous gardener who cycled in from an outlying village as occasion demanded, and that meant more or less full-time in the summer. The property testified to the commercial success of Leonard Appleton in a world not always kind to the conscientious and the self-deprecating. Rubber was his business, mainly for industry. Leonard – Len to virtually everyone except this chronicler – had made his way in the world, not through connexions, education or distinctive intelligence, but by dogged perseverance and resolute honesty, and the God he believed in seemed to have blessed his integrity with modest wealth, a favourable reputation and a pretty, vivacious wife. His wife was snatched from him in child-birth, and the loss nearly destroyed him, but for his daughter's sake he soldiered on, believing that he had a duty to her that no amount of self-pity should be permitted to override. His interests embraced golf – a weekly round with friends – international sport, particularly cricket, and sailing.

He could probably have afforded a governess or nanny for his daughter, but he was determined that no one would substitute for his wife in her or his own affections, and he juggled work and child-minders as best he could, bending his interests so that as much time as possible was spent on rearing his beloved child himself. Critics would point out that his business interests did not prosper as heretofore, on account of a loss of dynamism at the helm, but, provided that he maintained the company and the security of those who worked for it, he was unconcerned. What would expansion and growing wealth have brought him but greater troubles and less time available for his daughter? He preferred to cope with the present challenges than face new ones. His two sisters, Claire and Sarah, both younger than himself and with families of their own, were helpful in his support, and Leonard faced the future with – well, optimism would be an excessively strong word, but at least with confidence and hope that he could guide and sustain his daughter through her childhood and adolescence until a husband stepped in to claim her for his own.

The police inquiry into Leonard's murder drew a blank. Because there was no sign of forced entry, the investigators concluded that the murderer was known to his victim, but there was no record of an appointment at the house and no sighting of a visitor. (This was a tenuous argument, since Mr Appleton would not necessarily have locked his doors at the time of his killer's visit – whenever that was.) Tyre-marks in the drive were inconclusive. An inspection of the books revealed no anomalies, no suspicious associates, no suggestion of irregularity. Staff at the offices could shed no light on the matter, even though they were all individually interviewed, some more than once. The police went meticulously through the books to identify all contacts of Leonard Appleton in the course of his business. They investigated his contacts at the golf club-house and at the marina where his modest boat was moored. They combed his address-book and interviewed all those listed therein.

The inquiry focused naturally on acquaintances of Leonard Appleton who were familiar enough to use Christian names in their intercourse with the businessman. Two Micks emerged and were subjected to extensive questioning. One, Mick Tintern, was a long-standing friend introduced by a golf-club acquaintance before Leonard's marriage to Miriam, who became an intimate of the household and well-known to little Rachel. Despite the fact that Rachel would have recognised his voice easily and immediately had he been the mysterious stranger at the heart of the terrible events of the night of Leonard's death, the police persevered in their attempts to challenge his alibi. Not even Inspector French could have succeeded there, however. The second Mick, Mick Slaughter, was a supplier with whom Leonard had frequent dealings: not precisely a friend but closer to him than some whom Leonard would have included in his acquaintanceship. Mr Slaughter, having never, on his own testimony, visited the Appleton household, qualified for the police requirement that Rachel would not recognise his voice, but his character spoke vigorously in his favour. He had never brought himself to the notice of the forces of law and order, he had an unsullied reputation in the community, he was active in the structure of several local charities and of his local church. In short, the police found it impossible to cast him in the role of midnight strangler.

One thoughtful policeman suggested that the child had perhaps mistaken Dick, Nick, Rick or Vic for Mick, but, worthy and ingenious though this suggestion was, it produced no more positive result. Although Leonard Appleton knew several Richards, only one was ever addressed as Dick by those who knew him, and he had a perfectly satisfactory alibi, and none was addressed as Rick. The solitary Nicholas appeared not to fit the bill, either: an elderly acquaintance more or less house-bound since an accident in his seventy-fifth year, and in no position to be gallivanting about the countryside committing murder. The police interviewed a Victor Napier, but he was excluded on the basis of a satisfactory alibi.

To the credit of the local police force, they never closed the investigation but allowed two years to elapse before renewing their inquiries of Rachel, now in the eighth year of her age. She had moved in with her aunt and her aunt's children, had settled into her new school, seemed gradually to be forgetting the pain of her father's death. The police-woman, questioning Rachel at her new home one evening, did not remind the girl of the details of the event. She was tempted, for example, but resisted the temptation, to remind her that she had been found clinging to her father's dead body when the char-lady reported for work the following morning, in an effort to coax her into summoning from the depths of her memory any words that might have been exchanged by her father and the visitor, or any detail of the stranger's appearance, or any other feature of that evening. Nothing availed. There was no use in losing patience. The pain had simply closed down all the child's mechanism of recall.

*R*achel grew up and matured. Fidelity to historical truth compels the comment that she was not an attractive child. There is no reference here to her outward appearance, which was average: a brown-haired teenager with brown eyes, snub nose, full lips, dimpled chin. The reference is rather to her inner self, which was sour. Adverse judgement on this should be tempered with the knowledge that life had deprived her early of both parents. Of course, in the grand scheme of things; if we bear in mind the primitive history of cave-people (for example) battling with adversity in all its forms; the blood-stained history of humanity from the first skirmishes and wars to the bloodshed of the twentieth century's two world wars (and sundry minor wars); if we remember the diseases, the epidemics and the plagues that have scarred the human race over the centuries and the millennia; if we bear in mind the huge spread of humanity in time and space, with its diverse cultures and societies: losing both parents by the age of five is not an excuse for sourness of temperament. Many other children lose their parents young and grow up to be model citizens and exemplars of grace and charity and benevolence. However, trauma affects people in different ways. It is not for the outsider to sit in judgement on an individual and dictate the limits of the effect of trauma. It is for the individual to come to terms with the shock and absorb it into a wider framework of character and human interaction. The individual's response is going to depend on factors beyond the awareness of even the most skilful psychoanalyst, possibly beyond the awareness of the person most intimately concerned, and the stranger is better advised to seek understanding and tolerance than to rise up in condemnation. This narrative adopts the following stance. Rachel's character is not our concern: she was as she was, and it is not our function to analyse and express our disapproval. On the other hand, her actions cannot be condoned, and this narrative will not conceal its distaste. I suppose one should add that her murder cannot be condoned either.

> Sweet rose, whose hue angrie and brave
>
> Bids the rash gazer wipe his eye:
>
> Thy root is ever in its grave,
>
> > And thou must die.

The fact remains that Rachel was a sour and morose teenager: not at all everybody's cup of tea. This did not prevent her from making friends or from doing well at school. She shared her father's sporting keenness; she liked English and history; she did well at French.

One day she had a revelatory conversation with her boyfriend, a spotty, spindly youth with few other friends, whose name was Nat. Since he concerns us at this point only as the recipient of a rare confidence on Rachel's part which will have a bearing on the development of this narrative, we refrain from further description of this unsavoury youth. The two were sitting on a park bench one summer's day, holding hands idly and gazing out towards the pond, where doting mothers were trying to prevent their offspring from flinging themselves into the water after the pieces of bread intended for the wildfowl. The occasional couple strolled quietly by, arm in arm or hand in hand. A walker with a dog on a lead; a woman pushing a pram; an old person shuffling under the weight of years: it was a typical scene in an English park on a Sunday afternoon.

'You never talk about your parents,' Nat said, by way of casual conversation.

'Nothing to say,' was the laconic reply.

'There must be something to say,' Nat insisted. 'Tell me about your mother.'

Rachel was silent.

'Go on,' said Nat. 'You must have had a mother. It can't hurt to talk about her.'

'Not much to say,' said Rachel. 'I never knew her. She died giving birth to me, and all I know about her is second-hand from my father and my two aunts. I've seen pictures of her, of course, but I can't say she's part of my life. I've come to regard my aunt Sarah as the closest I'll ever get to a mother, and that seems to do me.'

'What about your father, then?' Gauche teenagers are oblivious to the finer points of social intercourse, but then he was not, in this case, to know. Again, for a moment, Rachel said nothing. Her face became intent, concentrated.

'My father died when I was five,' she said at length, but even Nat, obtuse, lanky, awkward Nat, detected in these words a strange depth of emotion, which he described to himself as a combination of misery and potent resolve. Sensing the special nature of the feelings now absorbing Rachel, he said nothing.

'I was there when it happened,' she said, gazing at the horizon, her memories stirring afresh. 'I remember sitting on the stairs in my night-dress, shivering with cold and fright.'

'Fright?' said Nat. 'What was there to be frightened of?'

'I was frightened of the anger and the tension. I could feel them. Of course, I didn't analyse my feelings like that at the time.'

When she said no more, Nat prompted her. 'Go on,' he urged her quietly.

'I was woken by angry voices. I knew something was wrong, so I crept out of bed and sat at the top of the stairs. I could hear my father and another man almost shouting at each other. They were both – oh, I don't know – angry, worked up.'

'What were they angry about?'

'That's just it,' Rachel said. 'I've no idea. Either I didn't understand it, or I've forgotten it. All I remember is they were angry - with each other.'

'And then what?'

Rachel reached back in her memory. Silently she scanned the past. Hesitantly, she said: 'I heard a scuffle. Blows. Grunts. They were fighting, I think.'

'You think?'

'Well, I now have difficulty in distinguishing what I remember from what I've been told by my aunts. I don't know which is which.'

'Well, what do you think you remember?'

'There was a crash and sounds of what I took to be a tussle. Then silence. Then a man rushed out of the house and slammed the door behind him.'

'And what did you do?'

'Oh, Nat, I went down the stairs, one at a time, shaking with fright, and peeped into the living-room.'

'Yes?'

'I don't remember any more. I have a vague idea of Mrs Crampton coming in – she was the char-lady, I think - and of a strange person asking me all sorts of questions, but it's all a blur. My aunt Sarah took me home with her, and I've lived with her ever since.'

'But your aunt must have told you something.'

'She did – eventually. She told me that Dad wouldn't be coming back, that he was dead and had asked her to look after me.'

'And have you never learnt any more?'

'No, nothing.'

'Don't you want to know?'

'No, what good would it do? Dad's gone. Killed in a fight, I suppose.'

'Did the police ever catch the other man – the one who killed your dad?'

'No. My aunt has told me everything was done, but they had nothing to work on. They never found out who he was.'

'Can't you help them?'

'I've told you, Nat,' she said with mounting emotion, 'I don't remember anything – nothing useful, anyway.'

'But you just told me you remember seeing him leave the house.'

'I do, vaguely. But he was gone, just like that. There's absolutely nothing about him I remember. I couldn't describe a single thing about him – except his voice, of course. I can't describe it, exactly, but I remember it. I shall never forget it.'

'Have you told the police?'

'What good would that do? I can't give them a photograph of his voice! They're not to know what he sounded like.'

'But there must be some way of exploiting your memory of his voice.'

'Oh, there is.'

The tone in which Rachel spoke alerted Nat, slow, acne'd Nat, to the presence of a strange emotion in his girl-friend.

'What?' he asked after a moment.

She spun round on the bench and faced him squarely. 'Nat, you're not to tell anyone else what I'm going to tell you now. Promise?'

Taken by surprise, Nat none the less promised.

'I've got his voice in my head. I go over it again and again. I am absolutely certain I would recognise it if I heard it. So I have spent my teenage years listening for it. Let me tell you one thing I don't remember, Nat, from that night. When the man left the house, there was silence. If he'd gone off in a car, I'd have heard the car. Even if he'd parked at the end of the drive, I'd have heard it; but I didn't.'

'So?'

'So he came on foot or on a bicycle. That means he was local. That means I can find him.'

'But he may have moved away.'

'He may have, but if he'd moved away at the time, wouldn't it have looked suspicious? And then when the police investigation died down, he'd have felt safe enough not to move.'

'Yes,' Nat said doubtfully.

'So since I've been old enough to go out on my own, I sit in cafés, I walk the streets, I wait outside pubs, I hang around shops, knowing that one day I shall hear his voice.'

'And when you do?' Nat hardly dared ask.

'I shall have my revenge. Yes, one of these days, I shall hear his voice, and then I shall know what to do.'

One of those days, she did.

Three

Several years after the conversation recorded in the previous pages, Rachel was engaged in her customary listening exercise, seated with her (new) boyfriend in a public house.

> In gloomy night
> by Fafner's cave I wait,
> my ears alert,
> keeping careful watch.

She was listening to him as he recounted his experience as a spectator at the latest local football match, but always with half an ear on the conversations taking place at the tables around her, at the bar, in the room. This was habit with her, and Andy, to whom her secret had been imparted, took no notice. By this time she was a presentable young person in the fullness of her womanhood, marred only by a dour scowl playing on her forehead. She worked as librarian in the town library and, having moved out of her aunt's house some time previously, lived on her own in a flat not far from the town centre. She was pleasant enough to those who patronised the library: helpful, knowledgeable, patient, but her obsession with her father's killer lurked permanently beneath the surface of her social activities, and to some she might have appeared rather distant or, in modern parlance, switched off.

Andy worked in a baker's in the town, rising early to prepare the first loaves, the rolls and buns, the pastries, tarts and pies, and leaving in the afternoon so that the cleaners could tidy up the mess, wash down the floors and work-surfaces, clean the equipment. He had no specific academic qualifications but was possessed of sufficient native wit to make his modest way in the world as an independent and (reasonably) upright citizen. In appearance he was well-set, tidy, clean-shaven (his job more or less required it), with perhaps more of a paunch than was consistent with long-term good health. That, however, is not relevant to the purposes of this narrative.

He and Rachel had met at a mutual friend's, and their relationship had taken hold slowly, without the passion of obsession or flights of whimsy. Theirs was a comfortable partnership, not hasty or pressured, but mature and calm. Both families hoped that it might lead to a firmer commitment in the fullness of time.

This well-matched couple were, as I say, seated in a public house in the town centre when Rachel suddenly went rigid with attention. Her features became immobile; she visibly strained sight and hearing; Andy could feel the tension as she focused. Behind her, two men who had just entered the premises were standing at the bar awaiting their turn to be served. Neither presented any remarkable features: two middle-class men taking time off in the evening for a quiet drink in a convenient tavern. Andy was infected by Rachel's change of demeanour and, in his turn, focused on the two men, whom he could see where she could not.

'No, no,' one was saying, 'although I liked the look of it, I didn't think the engine sounded quite right. The mechanic was adamant that he'd given it a thorough overhaul and that it was perfectly trustworthy, but why go for a car I'm not totally happy with when there are so many on the market?'

That was clearly not the voice which riveted the young woman seated just behind them. The man's companion answered.

'Quite agree with you. Might as well get something you feel comfortable with. I like my present car, but it's coming to the end of its useful life, and I'm thinking to upgrade to match my growing prosperity!'

'And I suppose you'll be looking for a bigger house as well!'

'Well, now you mention it … No, seriously, I don't think I'll move. I know the neighbours, the house suits me, and I don't think I could face the upheaval. The future of business under this Tory government is so uncertain I wouldn't risk very much. Buy a bigger house, and you find yourself saddled with a helluvalot of outgoings you can't afford.'

'It's psychological, you know. Unemployment topping a million: that speaks more to the heart than the head.'

'That's as may be, old boy, but the whole situation is so unpredictable I'd be a fool to splash out now. Perhaps next year, who knows?'

'Right, gentlemen, what'll it be?' came briskly from behind the bar.

The two men ordered and after a few minutes' silent wait wandered off to a corner of the saloon bar, visible to the young couple but out of earshot.

Rachel could hardly contain herself.

Is a light glittering there?

Nearer and nearer

it seems to shine;

it runs like a fiery steed,

breaks through the wood,

rushing this way.

Can it be he I'm waiting for?

'That's him!' she managed to say in an undertone, her voice containing triumph, relief, venom and expectation in equal measure. 'That's him! After all these years of waiting, I've finally got him!' She was clearly overwhelmed by the realisation that twenty years of her life were reaching a unique and pregnant moment. She shifted round so that she could look at the man squarely. As he was by now seated, it was difficult for her to judge his height, but Andy, having seen him standing at the bar, estimated five foot ten or eleven. The man was broad-shouldered, in his fifties, moustached, thin-lipped; affluent and self-confident. Rachel could not deflect her eyes from her father's murderer, the evil man who had destroyed her life, the reptile whose violence had obtruded itself to such terrible effect in the life of an innocent girl. She told Andy to drink in his appearance, to imprint it indelibly on his memory, so that no detail should be lost. She could not calm down. She brought a little relief by disappearing to the ladies'. When she re-emerged, she approached the bar casually, ordered another round for her and Andy, and asked, with what she hoped was becoming female nonchalance, whether the barman knew the two gentlemen who had just sat down in the corner.

'Well, not to say as know exactly,' was the reply. 'They come in once a week, presumably on their way back home from the office. Work round the corner in the Barford Buildings, I think. Something to do with insurance, are they? Not sure. That'll be just thirty p, please, love.'

Rachel was jubilant, although her sense of triumph and exhilaration was tempered by the thought that there was still a long way to go. She needed a name, an address, a knowledge of his family circumstances, familiarity with his daily routine. She needed time to plan her strategy, to think it through meticulously in the light of her further information. Screwing her courage to the sticking post was not the problem; getting her scheme absolutely right, so that she was not pinched in the movement but survived to pursue the second stage, was.

Her impatience was such that the following day she approached her manager.

'Mrs Jewel,' she said, 'you know there are three days of holiday owing to me. Would it be convenient to take them now?'

'What, this very minute?'

'Well, no,' said Rachel, 'but as soon as possible.' The manageress was reluctant to concede the request, as is the wont of many managers loath to yield the employees their rights. Having consulted the schedules, however, she agreed that Rachel could take the rest of the week off, starting from that evening.

The following morning, Rachel dressed inconspicuously, without make-up, in greys of various degrees, determined not to draw attention to herself in any way if at all possible. She stationed herself in the street opposite the entrance to Barford Buildings, leaning in a sequestered doorway, and she waited. Time passed, and there were to'ings and fro'ings as the building cranked itself up for the day's business, but there was no sign of her prey. She continued to wait, mulling over the circumstances which might have kept him from attending the office that day: illness? domestic upheaval? an accident? a family tragedy? she traversed the entire gamut of possibilities - until she realised her mistake. It was clear, as she thought through her failure, that Mr Villain would have driven straight to the back of the building, parked in the staff car-park and entered by a rear entrance. She had been waiting in the wrong place.

The following morning, therefore, she renewed her vigil, but this time standing in a back lane which gave access to the staff car-park. Here she found camouflage more difficult, but her supposition was that she would not have to wait for long. As she watched, close to the road, a Humber Sceptre (Mark III, although that was a detail that escaped her) turned the corner and entered the car-park at the back of the Barford Buildings. At its wheel sat her intended   victim. Pretending to notice nothing, she unwound and strolled off towards the front of the building, taking her time. She mounted the front steps and approached the reception desk.

'Excuse me,' she said to the middle-aged woman sat – perhaps slumped would be a more appropriate word – behind the counter, 'I'm looking for the owner of a silver Humber Sceptre who works in this building. You haven't seen him this morning, I suppose?'

'Now why would you be wanting to know that, young missy?'

'Well, you see, I was waiting at the lights just now and a cyclist came up on the inside and scratched the side of my car with his pedal. Before I could do anything, the lights turned to green, and the cyclist shot off. But I think your Humber Sceptre gentleman, who was waiting behind me, may have seen the incident and could help me out as a witness.'

'Hm,' the guardian of the building muttered, thumbing through a small file. 'That'll be Mr Napier. GFN 765C, was it?'

'Oh, I didn't have time to catch his number! Would he be likely to be coming out of the Worcester Road on to the High Street – you know, where that posh dress-shop is on the corner?'

'No, shouldn't think so, dear. He lives up Falkland Road somewhere – quite the opposite direction.'

'Oh, dear, then I've followed the wrong car. Never mind. Thanks very much for your help anyway. Bye-bye.'

She thought to herself that the extraction of the crucial information had been easier than anticipated.

Her next thought, to identify the house by consulting the telephone directory, proving unsuccessful, because no Napier living in Falkland Road was listed, she moved on to her next strategy:

another vigil. This, scheduled for a residential area, would prove a little trickier than her wait in a back street in the town centre, but she was not a whit deterred. She took up a studiedly casual stance at the end of Falkland Road, pretending to be awaiting a lift and looking regularly at her wrist-watch. In due course her patience was rewarded, when a silver Humber Sceptre came down Davies Road, negotiated the mini-roundabout and entered Falkland Road. To her discouragement, it then turned almost immediately left into Hazel Avenue and disappeared from view. By the time she had walked to Hazel Avenue, all trace had gone: Mr Napier had presumably garaged his vehicle or driven into one of the cul-de-sacs that lead off that road. She had no alternative but to renew her watch the following day, this time sitting on a low wall conveniently placed (for her purposes) near the corner of Hazel Avenue. To her satisfaction, the Humber swept into Hazel Street and then took the first left into Poplar Close. After a few yards' walk, she was rewarded with the sight of the driver emerging from his garage, closing the door behind him and entering his house by the front door, using a latch-key. There was no light in the house, suggesting, she thought, that he lived alone, except that was an over-optimistic conclusion not yet warranted by the evidence.

The next few weeks were a weary watch on the Barford Buildings and 5 Poplar Close, staked out from a variety of vantage-points. Andy was drafted in as auxiliary, taking over odd shifts, partly to give variety to her 'work', as she thought of it, partly to obviate the suspicions of local residents. Whoever the watcher, a note-book was at the ready to record times, and bicycles played an important part in following up sightings. The pair succeeded in building up a rough picture of the routine followed by their quarry. Saturday mornings were shopping day in the town. Sunday mornings saw Mr Napier at the Baptist Church and afternoons in the Malvern Hills. Monday, Wednesday and Thursday evenings were spent at home. Mr Napier permitted himself an hour or so in a pub, the Golden Wheatsheaf, on Tuesday evenings, as the young couple had discovered for themselves. That time may have been dictated by Napier's companion. Friday evenings, Napier attended a choir practice at the premises rented by the South Worcestershire Operatic Society, and Saturday evenings he was generally to be found dining out with friends, male and female.

It was difficult, on the basis merely of external observation, to build up a picture of Mr Napier as a person, and Rachel expanded their work by 'asking around'. They knocked on neighbours' doors, pretending to have found Mr Napier not at home and then making general conversation artfully steered. They returned to the Golden Wheatsheaf and sat with the other locals. They engaged the newsagent and the chemist and the grocer in conversation and gleaned snippets of information here and there. On the face of it, Mr Napier was an unlikely murderer. He was born in Worcester, went to local schools, joined an insurance firm at the bottom and worked his way up: nothing untoward, nothing that might agitate a researcher; a divorcee with no children. His interests were music, gardening and reading – all undeniably serious, educated and perfectly legal pursuits. He had friends, both singles and couples. He was to all intents and purposes a law-abiding and tranquil citizen, an example to the young and an asset to British society. As a younger man, however, he had strangled a friend in a fit of temper and orphaned his daughter. For that, full revenge must be exacted.

When she felt confident that the necessary steps had been taken, Rachel proceeded to enact the first part of her strategy. She bought an erotic photograph of a provocatively dressed (that is to say, a provocatively undressed) model, popped it into an envelope and posted it to Mr Napier, of 5 Poplar Close. Two days later, she gave him a telephone-call one evening, from a public kiosk in the town.

'Hi, Michael, is that you?'

'Who is that speaking, please?'

'It's Angèle, Michael. I sent you my photo two days ago.'

'I see.' Mr Napier was clearly at a bit of a loss. 'What can I do for you?' he eventually managed to say.

'I wonder whether we could meet.'

'Meet? But I don't know you!'

'That's the point, you darling man. I felt it was time we got to know each other. How about it?'

'Er, I don't know.'

'Go on, give it a try. If we don't get on, we need never meet again.'

'How do you know who I am?'

27

'I've seen you around and decided that you're my kind of man. I persuaded your newsagent, with a bit of a lie, I'm afraid, to give me your name and address, and here we are.'

'Oh, I don't – '

'Look, let's meet once and see how we get on. What do you say?'

Michael Napier struggled within himself.

'Well …'

'Excellent, that's the spirit. Look, do you know the Black Lion in Rynal Street? I'll meet you outside at six o'clock tomorrow night. Is it a deal? If you're not there, I shall be very disappointed. I'll have a nice meal ready round at my place, and we can make an evening of it together. Ooh, I'm so looking forward to it!'

The following evening – it was a Thursday, early closing – Rachel and Andy stationed themselves at either end of a snicket that ran between The Hodges, which was a cul-de-sac, and the High Street. At the High Street end, the snicket debouched next to a jeweller's. Andy was wearing an overcoat similar to the one worn by Napier that morning when he went to work, as observed by Rachel. At the Rynal Street entrance to The Hodges, Rachel, having checked that her victim was waiting outside the public house as agreed, signalled to Andy that all was ready. The next event was over in a few seconds. When Andy thought the appropriate moment had arrived - making sure he was seen by at least somebody, but not within sight of someone who could catch up with him as he ran - he smashed a brick through the window of the jeweller's, scooped up a handful of watches and made for the snicket as fast as his legs would carry him. As he passed Rachel, he dropped the watches into a bag she was holding, exited through The Hodges, turned left, took his overcoat off and placed it over his arm, and walked at a normal pace back to the High Street down Leicester Grove. For her part, Rachel walked up the remaining yards of The Hodges and turned right into Rynal Street. She approached Michael Napier waiting patiently and dutifully outside the Black Lion.

'Hello, Michael,' she said. 'It's lovely to see you. Thank you so much for turning up.' Before he could say anything in reply, she added, 'Just hold my parcel for me, will you, I'm going to dash into the ladies'. Be back in a couple of minutes.'

On the utterance of these words, she disappeared into the front entrance of the public house, came immediately out of the side door into The Hodges and made her way down the snicket towards the High Street. As she did so, two policemen came running up from the High Street, thrust past her and disappeared into Rynal Street with a squealing of whistles. Task accomplished, she met Andy sauntering down the High Street, and they walked off arm in arm to celebrate their victory.

Mr Michael Napier could not persuade the policeman at the station, after his arrest, that he had been led into a trap by an unknown girl. The photograph of her that he was finally allowed to produce in his defence was eventually identified as that of a London model who was miles away at the time of the crime. A witness was discovered who testified that he had seen a man of Napier's build and wearing a particular overcoat throw the brick and attempt to escape up to Rynal Street. That the thief had there stopped running was interpreted as a ruse to deflect the policemen's suspicion: the human equivalent of playing possum. To clinch his guilt, the watches were found on his person. There could be no doubt that the law had found its man.

It was, in criminal cant, a stitch-up, but once caught in its coils, Michael Napier was unable to extricate himself from the law. He was sent to prison for six months. That gave Rachel the breathing-space required to prepare for the second phase of her plan. When a week or so had passed, she persuaded Andy, to whom she was now affianced, to engage in a spot of house-breaking. She reasoned that nobody had only one set of house-keys; that Napier would naturally have taken one set with him to prison when he locked the house up preparatory to spending time as a guest of Her Majesty; and that that meant that a second set was sitting in his house, probably accessibly in case of an emergency. The first set would include his car-keys and perhaps keys to his office or to a filing cabinet therein. The second set would contain only those for the house, and perhaps only one of those. Andy gained entry by breaking a small pane of glass in the French windows at the back, inserting a gloved hand and turning the key, carelessly left in the lock. If entry had not been so easy that way, he had come prepared to use heavier methods. Once inside the house, he began his search in the hall, then moved to the kitchen, where he was lucky enough to find the object of his search. He checked that the key worked, closed and locked the French window, taking the precaution of measuring the broken pane of glass, and left by the front door, disturbing nothing else. The following day he had a copy made at a shoe-repairer's shop in Worcester, waited a further fortnight and then returned the key to its usual place, at dead of night but with sufficient boldness to assuage the suspicions of any onlooker, should there be one lurking in the road at that unlikely hour. Working quietly, he removed the remnants of the broken pane and reglazed the square. Rachel had convinced him that it was highly unlikely anyone would hear or see him. If Mr Napier had a friend calling in every so often, to check the house over during his enforced absence, a new pane of glass would less probably call attention to itself than a broken window. Furthermore, nothing in the house would seem to have been disturbed. There was some risk of discovery, of course, but Rachel - and Andy with her - were playing for high stakes.

Mindless of the Psalmist's apostrophe to the Godhead, 'May my vindication come from you', she was now ready for phase two of her revenge. She could afford to sit back a little until the release of Mr Napier from prison.

Four

*T*his second phase was a good deal trickier and more fraught with danger for herself and Andy than the first, which she viewed as a dummy run for the real business of entrapping her victim. On the other hand, laying her father's spirit to rest by punishing his killer was an imperative from which she did not shy, whatever the cost to herself. She had not read Book II of The Aeneid, either in the original or in any of the English translations available, but she was sufficiently attached to her father's memory to imitate, unknowingly, the pietas exemplified in Aeneas' rescue of the ancient Anchises as they fled from the burning ruins of Troy. Nor, regrettably, had she heard of the Roman emperor Antoninus, nicknamed Pius because of his dutiful remembrance of his adoptive father Hadrian. She might easily have argued, as some do, that one owes one's parents nothing, since life is not a favour accorded but a burden imposed. If anything, parents should be grateful that their offspring do not promptly cast the gift of life back in their face.

Her survey of suitable premises in the town persuaded her that the Worcestershire Building Society branch in Oat Street would best suit her purposes. She and her husband Andy decided, after considerable discussion, to adopt the same tactics as before. They reasoned that the building society would recover all its money, and the shock administered to the counter staff would pass. The society would therefore suffer no damage in the long term. Michael Napier, on the other hand, would suffer no more than he deserved.

They satisfied themselves, first of all, that Napier was out of prison, back at home and back at his job. How he managed this third feat was no concern of theirs. They satisfied themselves, secondly, that he had resumed his regular life-style and was spending an hour after work in the Golden Wheatsheaf on Tuesdays, mulling over the vagaries of human life with his friend. Suitable weather conditions would be rain on a Tuesday evening in winter, when fewer people would be in the streets, and these conditions did not prevail to her satisfaction until a week in mid-January, when Rachel thought that the time had arrived for her plans to mature. She and Andy agreed on their plan of campaign, met at lunch-time to finalise their movements and returned to their respective places of work preparatory to the events of the late afternoon.

It is not to be thought that Rachel was cavalier or relaxed at the thought of what she, through her devoted husband, was about to attempt. There was a tightening in her stomach, a constriction in her breathing, as she thought of the risks. Although she had had upwards of twenty years to think, to determine the proper course of action, to examine her plan from every point of view, including ethical, now that the moment of reckoning was on her, her resolution was tested. She had discussed it with Andy, but he, poor soul, was besotted with her in a quiet sort of way and had neither the training nor the inclination to rehearse the moral arguments that might be advanced against the proposed course of action. He had his share of courage and enterprise, and if Rachel required of him tasks that would have daunted a lesser man, his was not the temperament to impede the implementation of her revenge. It is idle to speculate what alternatives he might have considered if he could have foreseen, in the tea-leaves, perhaps, or in the entrails of a sacrificed sheep, the results of Rachel's plotting.

Speed was essential. The amount of money seized was immaterial. Having agreed to go ahead, their separation after lunch meant that there could be no turning back if their relationship and Rachel's scheme were to survive. If Rachel reneged, her chances of getting assistance from her help-meet in future were slim. If, on the other hand, Andy lost his nerve, it is unlikely that Rachel would simply have clasped him lovingly to her bosom and continued as before. Perhaps the element of risk stimulates some to attempt feats of daring closed to the more cautious. Life is littered with examples of risk-taking that are beyond the comprehension of the pedestrian and the prosaic.

32

Again aping Napier's overcoat of the morning, Andy donned a mask, hurtled into the building society premises, brandished a replica gun and demanded the day's takings. The staff hesitated. One he could see pressing the alarm button. None of this mattered. He grabbed what he could from behind the counter and fled up Oat Street. Just out of sight, standing in Cowl Street, Rachel was waiting with an open bag, into which the faithful husband dropped the cash and the imitation gun before disappearing across the road into Nightingale Court and through the alley into Mill Street, where he adopted a casual walk. Rachel walked slowly into Chapel Street, a law-abiding citizen about to take up a rendezvous with her affectionate husband.

A week later, when the weather was dry, Rachel set off to Napier's house to plant, at the bottom of the wardrobe in one of his spare bedrooms, the imitation gun and the cash from the building society premises. She told Andy she would telephone the police from a call-box on her way back to meet him in town for a celebratory supper, to tell them, anonymously it goes without saying, that the money taken from the Worcestershire Building Society the previous week could be found, if they cared to look, at No.5 Poplar Close.

When she failed to keep her appointment at the Happy Haddock in the High Street, Andy was a little perturbed. He waited. He waited another while. Eventually, he went home to await her there, wondering what could have caused the change of plan. Instead of planting the building society cash on Napier, perhaps she had absconded to start a new life for herself? The idea was ridiculous, partly because Andy and she were, as far as he could tell, perfectly happy together, and partly because the cash was totally insufficient for such a purpose. Perhaps, on the other hand, she had met a friend and had decided to have supper in town with her – or with him. That, however, would have been a distinctly odd proceeding. Perhaps, thirdly, she had had an accident and was in hospital. In that case, he reasoned, somebody in authority would have got in touch with him, since the contents of Rachel's handbag would readily have identified her. He was still puzzling over her absence when he decided to go to bed for the night, determined to take further, and more strenuous, steps in the morning, when he could rationally exclude any but grave reasons for her not returning home. Andy was not a complicated soul. He took life as it came, refusing to ask questions that could not, from a Marxian perspective if he had but known it, be answered, happy to accept his lot as destiny had preordained, and confident that, willingly adopting the place in the world to which his birth, upbringing, intelligence, skills and personality had assigned him, he would fulfil his role in the grand scheme of things without further effort on his part.

On the following day, he asked and received permission from his manager to stop work briefly at nine o'clock in order to telephone his wife's place of work. He explained that he was worried over her failure to return home the previous night and had not raised the alarm in case, there being a perfectly natural explanation, he made a fool of himself and wasted police time. When he returned from his telephone-call, however, the manager could see from the expression on his youthful face that she had not turned up for work, and he therefore suffered the distressed youth to inform the police that his wife was inexplicably missing. He suggested that Andy took the day off so that he could assist the police in their search.

A Constable Ridley called at the house to take particulars.

'What is your wife's full name, Sir?' the constable began.

'Rachel Wendy Carver,' he said.

'Age?'

'Twenty-seven.'

'Description?'

'Here, Constable, take this photo. That's probably better than my trying to describe her.'

'A good idea, Sir.'

'Any distinguishing features?'

'Well, no, not really, unless you count a large mole on her right shoulder-blade.'

The constable, deciding that that feature was worth making a note of, scribbled in his note-book.

'Now, Sir, tell me about the last time you saw her and when you began to get worried.'

'Well, Constable, Rachel works at the public library in Oat Street. On a Tuesday, she leaves work at four o'clock. She wished to do some shopping in town but had forgotten her cheque-book. So she came home first and set off again, saying that she would meet me at a quarter to six at the Happy Haddock in the High Street and we would have a fish supper for a change. I set off to meet her, got to the restaurant a few minutes before the agreed time and sat down to wait. She never turned up.'

'And why did you wait until the morning to phone us, Sir?'

Andy gave his reasons, and Constable Ridley seemed satisfied. The policeman assured Mr Carver that he would immediately set the appropriate wheels in motion to discover his wife's present whereabouts. The police would circulate her photograph, inquire of hospitals, check for sightings of distressed females, contact neighbouring forces: all the usual steps.

As is well known, thousands of people disappear each year. Most, it seems, choose to do so, the reasons being as diverse as the situations from which people wish to escape. The hardship lies with those left behind, in ignorance and uncertainty and trepidation. The constable explained all this to Andy Carver. He asked in particular whether Carver was aware of any problem or threat from which his wife would like to have fled.

'No, Constable, absolutely not. I have had time to ask myself these questions. There is no domestic or family crisis, no financial difficulty, no health scare that I can think of which would have precipitated any sort of disappearance. Rachel has two aunts she is close to and four cousins on that side. I have phoned them without success. She has several close female friends, and they know nothing either. I am completely baffled.'

'If your wife were looking for a few days' rest or retreat – I don't say she is, Sir, I'm only asking: if she were – where is she likely to go?'

'Her aunt Sarah, I suppose, who brought her up from the age of five.'

'What if she decided on a hotel? Would she be able to afford it?'

'Well, she had her purse and her cheque-book with her, so, yes, I suppose she would have enough money to stay at a hotel if she wished to.'

'I'm sorry to ask this question, Sir, but would there be any male friend who might have given her sanctuary?'

'No, Constable. I told you, our marriage is a perfectly happy one. In any case, I don't know of any male friend close enough to her.'

The constable was aware that husbands who have done away with their wives often contact the police with a story of a missing wife, because it would seem unnatural and suspicious not to do so. Constable Ridley was reasonably sure that Andrew Carver was sincere, but one could never be sure. Still, it would be advisable to bear in mind that big insurance pay-outs could play a part in human dramas like the one playing itself out before him. There were, moreover, many other reasons why a man might wish to rid himself of his wife – or, conversely, a wife of her husband, although that was not at issue here. Constable Ridley reminded himself that marriage was the most difficult human relationship to sustain and that even small obices could create major tensions.

Thoughtfully the constable made his way back to the station to begin the process of search. He disliked this one aspect of his job. It was not that the procedures were complex or particularly difficult, or that they involved danger or personal loss – he was not being asked to enter unarmed the house of a crazed gunman or to intervene in a pub brawl - but so often they ended in tears by bringing to light a murder, an abduction, a broken family, a relationship on the rocks: almost inevitably, even if the missing person were found, a failure of some sort in a world already full of failure and heartache. He had only just begun to initiate inquiries when a report came in that a woman's body had been found behind the Baptist chapel in Seward Close, off Cowl Street. He was invited to attend the scene with a police photographer and to make an appropriate report. He hurried out to the scene of the discovery, to find a person whom he took to be, and later discovered to be, the caretaker. The simple story was that the caretaker had made his weekly trip to the back of the church premises to check the boiler-house and had stumbled on the body lying between the building and the boundary hedge. He had immediately returned home, which was only just down the road, to report his find, before returning to the church to await the arrival of the police. He could see at a glance that an ambulance was not what was required.

After taking down the caretaker's statement and allowing the photographers to record the scene for the coroner, and for the murder team when such should be in place, he sent a radio message to the station, asking for the body to be removed for autopsy. Even PC Ridley, inexperienced as he was, could recognise a fatal bullet-wound in the chest when he was faced with one.

The astuteness of the station sergeant led to a connexion between this murder and the raid on the Worcestershire Building Society of the week before. An anonymous telephone-call to the police station on the previous night had invited the authorities to search the premises known as No.5 Poplar Close if they wished to discover evidence of the armed raid. Three policemen had accordingly been detailed to call, armed with a search warrant, and they had found Mr Napier at home, not long returned from his weekly session at the Golden Wheatsheaf and about to prepare his solitary supper. He had protested his innocence of all crime but allowed the police to proceed with their search, on the grounds, repeated to himself several times, that it was useless to attempt to prevent them. He stood by helplessly as the men searched his home, soiling it with their lack of concern and their official intrusion and their prurience. When the man in charge came down the stairs triumphantly waving a bag, the contents of which were declared to be building society material, including cash, and a Browning revolver, Napier stood aghast, seemingly numbed into inactivity in his bewilderment. At first, as he professed later, he thought of accusing the police of planting the evidence in the attempt to gain a conviction for a crime of which he was wholly innocent, but he swiftly remembered his previous brush with the law and discerned a small pattern emerging, in which police dishonesty did not figure.

The sergeant was fully aware that guns did not occur frequently in his domain, and yet a victim of gun-crime and a gun had appeared in the same night. He could not fail to draw a conclusion. To his satisfaction but not to his surprise, the dead woman proved to have been shot at close range by a Browning 9 mm Hi-Power semi-automatic pistol, the very weapon found at Mr Napier's premises. The Hi-Powers had been produced in their thousands and tens of thousands over several decades, changing little either in appearance or in mechanism, although various models were introduced, but laboratory tests showed beyond a peradventure that Napier's gun – so the police labelled it – was the weapon involved in the young woman's death.

It did not take the police long, either, to connect the discovery of the body with Mr Andy Carver's report of the previous day. The case looked at first sight straightforward. Despite possible appearances to the contrary, Napier was undoubtedly a criminal, sent down for robbery after due process of law. He had graduated from a relatively minor smash-and-grab raid to armed robbery and now to murder. For some reason yet to be clarified, the deceased Mrs Carver had fallen foul of Napier, and he had used on her the self-same weapon with which he had threatened the building society staff, dumping her body in a secluded spot before returning to his house for supper – and an unexpected encounter with three policemen in connexion with a week-old crime. The connexion between Michael Napier, divorced businessman recently out of prison, and Rachel Carver, librarian and married woman half his age, that led the former to kill the latter, would indubitably emerge in the course of even superficial inquiries. On the other hand, there were, as was only to be expected so early in the case, aspects to be clarified. There was no doubt about that. For example, Napier doubtless had unbreakable alibis to cover his time at work, his short walk to the Golden Wheatsheaf and his hour there. Would he really have had time between his session at the public house and the police visit to kill a woman and return home to cook his supper, leaving no trace of the murder on his clothes? His sequence of actions, as he enumerated them in defiance of appearances, would have to be closely scrutinised. Why, further, would he hide the cash and gun in so obvious a place as a wardrobe in his spare bedroom? Would it not have been much safer to discard the gun and throw away anything apart from old notes that could have enabled anyone to make a connexion between the building society that suffered the raid and the booty? Perhaps the mysteries were superficial and trivial, but one could never be sure. No, all in all, this was a case for Inspector Wickfield.

Stanley Wickfield – Stan to his wife, his colleagues and his friends – was an experienced detective with a number of successful investigations to his credit. His superiors were sometimes impatient with his, as they saw it, ponderous deliberation. His colleagues sometimes regarded him as soft, even anodyne. His assistants and the public, on the other hand, had every reason to be grateful for his courtesy, his lack of side, his tact. What was not in doubt was the incisiveness of his intelligence once he had assembled the essential materials of a case. He might have been slow – 'bumbling' in the offensive terminology of his envious rivals - but he was invariably successful, and many criminals had regretted locating their nefarious activities in Worcestershire. He spent his spare time reading, gardening, walking, listening to music; idyllically happy with his wife of thirty years, Beth, and proud of his two sons, now both away from home engaged in careers of their own. He attempted DIY operations round the house and liked to do the cryptic crossword each night, if he were home. His superiors considered him to be ideal to take on the case of the furacious businessman and the murdered Mrs Carver.

Five

Wickfield began by reviewing the few facts in the case of the death of Rachel Carver. On the morning of Wednesday 9 December, the caretaker of the Baptist chapel had found her body in the town. Death was caused by two gun-shot wounds to the chest administered approximately fifteen hours previously, and the gun used was discovered in the house of one Michael Napier, a local businessman, after a tip-off. As well as the gun, cash stolen from a building society in the town the previous week was found in Napier's house. At first hearing the facts spoke for themselves, but Wickfield's responsibility was to enable the police to proceed with a prosecution that would persuade a jury, and for that the facts had to be fleshed out.

'Spooner,' he said to his sergeant, 'I'd like you to come with me to interview this Michael Napier. He's obviously the key to the business. So grab your note-book, and we'll take a pot of tea with us, as I fear we shall be there some time. Interview Room 3: I'll meet you there in a few minutes.'

'Very well, Sir.'

Spooner had been Wickfield's chosen assistant for three years, and he would not have had it otherwise. He valued the weight that the inspector gave to his ideas and the manner in which he was treated more as a colleague than as an inferior. He was in his early thirties, still youthful, always smart and agreeable in appearance. His wife worked as a shop-assistant in Cannington, a small town a few miles outside the city boundary, and she was expecting their first child.

'Right, Mr Napier, this is Detective Sergeant Spooner, and my name is Wickfield. We hope between us to get to the bottom of this business, and I'm sure we can rely on your cooperation.'

'Inspector – I presume you are an inspector – you can't be keener than I am to clear up this mess. The whole thing is a ghastly mistake, and I blame myself partly for being such a fool in the first place.'

'"In the first place"? Would you like to explain that, Mr Napier?'

'Earlier this year, I was set up by a woman who planted on me the proceeds of a smash-and-grab raid at a jeweller's. You must have heard about it, Inspector?'

'No, sorry, I'm afraid not. I'm hardly ever called on to deal with - what shall we say? - minor crime. Tell us briefly what happened.'

'A woman arranged to meet me at a certain spot in town – outside the Black Lion in Rynal Street, it was. As I was waiting there, she thrust a parcel into my hand and scarpered, with the excuse that she was going to powder her nose in the pub behind us. A minute later, two policemen arrested me as I stood there with the parcel in my hand. No sign of the woman, of course.'

'And the parcel contained jewellery, I take it?'

'Yes.'

'Tell us about this woman.'

'There's nothing to tell! I caught just a faint glimpse of her – '

'No, I mean, start from the beginning. How had she got in touch with you?'

'She phoned me.'

'What, out of the blue?'

'Well – ' His hesitation was revealing.

'Look, Mr Napier, we need the whole story if we're going to be of any use here. Please don't start hiding things from us.'

'Oh, all right, Inspector, but you'll take me for a fool.'

'Mr Napier, we're not interested in how foolish people have been. Our job is crime, not foolishness.'

'I received a photo through the post – sort of pornography. It was of a young woman. No name, no letter, Worcester post-mark. Puzzling, but not particularly suspicious. Then a couple of days later, a woman claiming to be the sitter phoned, asking me to meet her.'

'Did she give a name?'

'No. No, wait a minute, she did: Angèle, I think. French, isn't it? But she sounded perfectly English.'

'What reason did she give for wanting to meet you?'

'Because I'm tall, dark and handsome. No, seriously, Inspector, that's more or less what she said. She said she'd seen me around, thought I was her kind of guy, found out who I was and phoned me.'

'And you accepted this?'

Napier stroked his moustache.

'Yes, why not? I'm divorced, no attachments. I've not taken a vow of celibacy, you know. And she also said that if we didn't get on at that first meeting, we should go our separate ways, no harm done. I did hesitate, but in the end I accepted her invitation.'

'And was this the same girl who gave you the watches?'

'Yes, I should say so. When I met her outside the pub, she spoke only a sentence or two, but yes, I'd say it was the same voice.'

'Did the police investigate this girl, do you know?'

'Well, I know they traced the girl in the photograph – some London model, I think; completely irrelevant, as far as they could make out.'

'OK, Mr Napier. Why should this girl be out to trap you? Her plan seems to have been to put you away for a time, or smear your name, or perhaps to punish you. Which, any idea?'

'No, no idea at all. The whole thing is a complete mystery to me – and don't think I haven't thought about it, because I have. I've turned over the possibilities in my head until I've nearly driven myself nuts.'

'What girls of that age do you know?'

'My brother has two girls in their twenties, and a couple of friends have girls in that age group too, but I'd have recognized all those, wouldn't I? I'm quite sure it was nobody I knew or had ever met – to the best of my recollection, anyhow.'

'Now think carefully, Mr Napier. Is there anything in your past where you might have caused damage or offence – enough for somebody to wish to get back at you?'

Napier sat for a moment in silence.

'Well, Inspector, I've done stupid things in the past, who hasn't? but there's absolutely nothing I can think of that would have caused this sort of upset.'

'Nothing at school or university?'

'Didn't make university, I'm afraid. But even if I had, this girl would be the same age as me, wouldn't she, and she was definitely half my age.'

'OK, Mr Napier, let's move on to the death of Rachel Carver. Did you know her?'

'Never heard of her, Inspector. That's the honest truth.'

'Did my colleagues show you a picture of her? Perhaps you knew her under another name.'

'No, I've no idea what she looked like.'

The team paused while Spooner went to fetch the photograph that her husband had brought in to the station for purposes of identification. Napier took the photograph solemnly and stared at it for a moment.

'No, Inspector, I've never seen this woman before. Mind you, it's not a particularly memorable face, is it, or perhaps I shouldn't say that. But no, I don't know her.'

'What were your movements on the night of her murder – the night before last?'

'Let me see. Tuesday? Well, on Tuesdays I always meet my pal Justin Blackwater for a jar at the Golden Wheatsheaf. Have done for years. So from work I walked straight up to the pub and sat with Justin for an hour. He's a friend from school, and we've kept up our friendship all these years. We don't discuss world problems very much, or engage in deep philosophical discussion, but we just enjoy each other's company for an hour a week. That's no crime, is it? Then I walked back to the office to get my car. Got home at I should think a quarter to seven, perhaps a little later, and I was just thinking about what to have for supper when three policemen burst in and ransacked the place. Well, I dramatise a bit, but that's what it felt like at the time. I've no idea what it's all about. So here I am, in a police cell, with my fate apparently in your hands, Inspector.'

'Have you any idea how the incriminating articles got into your house? If you didn't put them there, somebody else did. Who, when and how?'

'I've no idea, Inspector, absolutely none. I'm as much in the dark as you are.'

'Yes, thank you for that note of confidence, Mr Napier' – but he smiled as he said it. 'Who has a key to your house?'

'No one. I have two sets for myself, and that's it. Oh, and my brother has a front door key, but he doesn't need to use it very often, as I'm nearly always in when he calls.'

'And his two girls?'

'They come over regularly, but they always make sure I'm in first.'

'Yes, I see. Now is there anything else you'd like to tell us at this juncture? I must tell you that I'm inclined, personally, to accept your story, but there's some way to go before we can convince the powers that be that you had nothing to do with Mrs Carver's murder. You deny knowing her, but we can't be certain of that yet, can we? The gun that killed her was found in your house, along with the building society cash from the week before. They didn't get their on their own, you know, and you have no explanation. Now, is there anything you'd like to ask us? '

'Yes, Inspector, when can I get out of here?'

'Well, in view of the, er, circumstances, I'm sure we can arrange bail for you. We'll have you out in next to no time, you see if we don't, and thank you for being so cooperative. We shall need to see you again, though, so no disappearing off to the Balearics.'

Having concluded this interview to his satisfaction, Inspector Wickfield next took Spooner to interview the bereaved husband. Andrew Carver had requested time off work until after the funeral, and the detectives found him moping at home, still in a state of shock after his wife's death. The house was a modest terraced property off Greenhill to the north of the town, quiet enough if you discounted the noise from the adjacent railway line. Before it, behind a low brick wall, was a small front garden laid to paving with a few potted plants, looking less than their best under the late autumn sky. The curtains were clean, the front door was clean. The policemen's ring was answered shortly by a young man with an unexpressive face. Mousey hair was tousled. Its owner had clearly not shaved. Spectacles sat low on the bridge of his nose.

'May we come in, Mr Carver? We're police officers investigating your wife's death.'

Without looking at their badges, shown with circumspection for his attention, he led them into a back room which stood between the kitchen and the front hall. A coal fire was burning in a stove on one wall, while a settee occupied the opposite wall. There was a television set, a cabinet holding some glass, with, above it, a bookshelf stocked with reference-books, some novels, some romance. Through the open door, the detectives could see that the kitchen was tidy, apart from a small pile of cutlery and crockery which occupied the sink. Mr Carver had had the energy to eat – something at any rate - but not to do the washing-up.

'I told the police officers yesterday all I know,' he said with a trace of petulance.

'I am aware of that, Mr Carver, and we'd like to thank you for being so helpful at what must be a terrible time for you. You have our every sympathy in your loss, believe me.'

He paused. He and Spooner were seated on the sofa, while their host occupied an arm-chair by the fire. The room was, to Wickfield's taste, excessively warm, but he did not think that the interview would last long. He gazed at the picture above the fireplace: a still-life featuring some pheasants hanging over the edge of a table and a bowl of late-summer flowers. It would not be his choice for the room's focal-point.

'However, if we are to stand any chance of catching the murderer,' he went on, 'we must have as much information as possible, and what you may have told someone else is not sufficient. I hope you don't think me officious.'

'Oh, go ahead, Inspector.'

'First of all, then, I'd like you to tell me what your wife was doing in the town on Tuesday evening. She cannot have been attacked in the High Street, for example. Or let me rephrase that. It is very unlikely she was attacked in the High Street, because somebody was sure to have heard the shot. So where was she going?'

'She went out shopping, that's all. She left home at about a quarter past four and said she would meet me at the Happy Haddock in the High Street at a quarter to six. She never turned up, and that's all I know.'

'Which shops was she going to? What was she going to buy?'

'I think she was hunting for something for her aunt Sarah's

45

birthday, but that means she could have been anywhere: a lingerie shop, household goods, a delicatessen, a bookshop, who knows? She certainly never told me where she was going.'

'Now, Mr Carver, do you know of anyone who would wish your wife harm? We haven't found her handbag yet – she must have had one with her if she was shopping – but it doesn't seem very probable that someone shot her and dumped her body just to snatch her handbag. So: enemies?'

'I really don't know, Inspector. Do you think I haven't asked myself that question?'

'How long had you known Rachel?'

'A couple of years.'

'Do you know anything about previous boyfriends?'

'No, but the girls at Rachel's work might know.'

'What sort of family did she come from?'

'She was orphaned. Her mother died in childbirth, her father when she was five. She was brought up by her aunt Sarah.'

'In Evesham?'

'Yes. Well, Hampton: Evesham near enough.'

'Are there any brothers or sisters?'

'No, but she regarded her two cousins, children of her aunt Sarah, as her siblings, since she had lived with them from the age of five.'

'Any family feuds? arguments with neighbours?'

'I've told you, Inspector, I've no idea. I can't imagine who would wish Rachel harm.' Therewith he crumpled into a quiet sobbing.

Wickfield esteemed that a good moment to conclude their interview, which had yielded little new information, although one small nugget emerged later. He and Spooner let themselves out, and the former immediately suggested a call on aunt Sarah in an attempt to come to grips with Rachel's childhood. Neither of the men was particularly familiar with the Evesham area, and it took them a little time to work their way out to Hampton. They stopped on the way for a late lunch at the Hungry Fox. Normally Wickfield would have inquired of his assistant, at this or an equivalent point, what thoughts about the case had occurred to him, but on this occasion he was too preoccupied with his own thoughts. He was convinced that Rachel had been specifically targeted and was not the victim of a random killer or mugger, although he could not completely discount the possibility. Could he be certain that her husband knew nothing of such a person? If Andrew did know something but was concealing the information from the police, what could be his motive for such concealment? Was he himself the killer? Wickfield's questions set in train a number of speculations which kept him busy over lunch.

In due course, the pair located aunt Sarah's residence at the far end of Evendene Road, well away from any traffic passing on the B4084. Aunt Sarah, a buxom woman in her early fifties, was not surprised to find two policemen on the doorstep. The house was a detached property known to estate agents the land over as a villa. This one was not sumptuous but comfortably middle-class. Mrs Platt received them mutedly but pleasantly and surmised that they had called about her niece's death.

'What else, I'm afraid, Mrs Platt? A very sad business. Please accept our sincere condolences.'

'I feel so terrible, Inspector. Rachel was like a daughter to me. To have died would have been bad enough, but to be murdered! What can it all be about?'

When the small party were seated in the living-room and refreshments had been offered and refused, Wickfield began slowly with several statements and a question.

'We think your niece was specifically targeted, Mrs Platt. In other words, this wasn't a random killing. That means that she had an enemy hating her enough and determined enough to wish to do away with her. What we need to know from you is who that person might be. So can you tell us if Rachel had any enemies that you know of?'

'Inspector, I've known Rachel since she was born. There isn't a gentler, kinder creature in the world. No one could wish her harm.'

'Mrs Platt, I'm very glad to hear you say so, but the fact is that someone has shot her. So there is at least one enemy out there, and it's my job to find out who it is.'

'In that case, Inspector, I can't help you, but I can tell you that I haven't been so upset since her father's death all those years ago.'

'Quite, Mrs Platt. He can't have been very old.'

'Thirty-five. They never caught him, you know.'

'"They never caught him." Whom did they never catch, Mrs Platt?'

'The murderer, of course.'

'What? Her father was murdered?'

'You must remember the case, Inspector. 1951, February. Len was found strangled in his own sitting-room, with the child clinging to his body, and although there was an extensive police investigation, the killer was never found.'

'This is very interesting, Mrs Platt. No, I knew nothing about it, but in 1951 I was living in Warwickshire, miles away, so perhaps that's not surprising. Please tell me what happened.'

Mrs Platt entered into a long and detailed account of the murder and of the inquiry that followed.

'Now that could shed a whole lot of light on Rachel's murder,' Wickfield said. 'I'm extraordinarily grateful to you, Mrs Platt, for telling me all this. I had no idea. I had presumed that your brother's death accounted for your taking Rachel in, but the circumstances come as a complete surprise to me. I have to say that this puts quite a different complexion on things.'

At this point Spooner intervened.

'Mrs Platt,' he said, 'although the police never identified your brother's murderer, did you, do you, have any suspicions yourself? Perhaps there was a chief suspect but no evidence against him?'

'No, Sergeant,' she said, as she turned to face him, 'I knew of absolutely no one who bore Len a grudge. As far as I could see, the police at the time did all they could. The only real clue was that Rachel remembered her father calling his visitor "Mick", but that clue came to nothing in the end. I have always imagined that Rachel misheard. Perhaps Len said something like, "I'm not that thick" or "Surely you didn't fall for that trick" or "He dropped a brick", or any one of hundreds of other phrases, and Rachel simply misunderstood. She was only five, you know, not in the same room, and had just been woken up. I never took her so-called memory seriously, but I suppose the police felt they had to follow it up in case there was anything in it.'

The conversation with Mrs Platt continued for some time, as the detectives tried, in vain, to uncover other sinister events in Rachel's childhood and adolescence. Her father's murder, dramatic enough by any standards, was the sole event that promised to shed light on the present, and it seemed reasonable to Wickfield – and to Spooner –

to take it as a starting point for their present investigation. Wickfield pondered the relationship between police investigations into murder and divine retribution. He was an active believer, and he had always understood from his catechism that malefactors brought punishment on themselves, in the next world if not in this, by choosing paths which destroyed the essence of what it means to be human. He did not share the mediaevals' crude image of an avenging Judge keen to mete out punishment for every misdeed, but he did believe that, for life to make any sense and for those who suffered injustice to be vindicated, there had to be some place or time of reckoning. Furthermore, he knew that all the world's major religions taught the same. How it might work out in practice he was content to leave to God. If the police failed to catch a miscreant and temporal punishment was thus evaded, the misdeeds would reap their own reward, sooner or later, and Wickfield was not going to give himself undue anxieties on the score. That did not lessen his determination to solve this crime, like all others submitted to him by his superiors, but it relieved him of undue sollicitude *sub specie aeternitatis.*

Six

*I*t was at this stage that Wickfield asked Spooner for the first time how he felt the case was shaping up.

'Shaping up, Sir? We're only just getting our heads round the facts! We can't theorise before we get the facts straight, Sir, you know that as well as I do.'

'I know, I know, Sergeant, but have a go anyway. We've never let the facts get in our way before, and I see no reason why we should start now.'

'Very well, Sir, but be it on your own head. Don't shoot me down for wild speculation.'

The pair were seated, as often on these occasions, in a public bar back in Worcester, a short distance from the police-station, cosseting alcoholic drinks of small strength. Because discretion was required, they frequented such establishments at quiet hours when they could be certain of occupying a cosy nook on their own, far from eavesdroppers (had anybody wished to eavesdrop, which was unlikely). Both men cherished these occasions, when rank seemed of little importance, the demands of superiors for instant results remote, and opportunities for flights of fancy and therefore for serendipity profuse. Often their cases progressed by the little steps established at such confabulations.

'Our recent chat with Mrs Platt was very helpful, Sir, don't you think?'

'It certainly was. The one thing that struck me was why young Andy Carver never mentioned to us the murder of Rachel's father.

He must know about it, and he must realise that it could have a direct bearing on the case.'

'Exactly what I was wondering myself, Sir. So why didn't he mention it?'

'The only reason I can think of is that he was frightened we'd discover something to his disadvantage. When are the public going to realise that we're not thought-police or morality-police and that the sooner the truth emerges, the sooner the case is solved?'

'My thoughts precisely, Sir. So what could he be frightened we'd discover?'

'He or Rachel or both were engaged in something underhand to do with the murder of Rachel's father, and they don't wish us to find out about it. Any ideas?'

'My guess, Sir, is that Rachel was the girl stringing Michael Napier along, but I'm not quite sure how that ties in with the murder of Len Appleton twenty years ago – unless, of course, she thought Napier was the murderer. How could she know that, though, when the police were baffled? She was five years old, for heaven's sake, and the police had at their disposal a sophisticated system of inquiry and search. If Andy, on the other hand, knows about the saucy photograph and the rest of it, perhaps he's ashamed, except that these days people don't seem to bother about shame very much.'

'Yes, Sergeant, I follow that, but who in your opinion shot Rachel, which is the real question facing us?'

'Well, Sir, there are only two suspects, Napier and Andy. Neither seems very likely to me.'

'No, I agree with you, but I think we need to investigate their alibis much more firmly: so far we've only taken their word for where they were at the time, and we don't yet know how much their word is worth. We have to bear in mind that neither is necessarily going to look or sound like a murderer, the sort of person you find in official police photographs, where the villain stares straight at you, low forehead, narrow eyes, the stubble of several days and a fearsome expression on his face. They're both obviously going to put their best side forward. And a secondary question is the robbery at the building society: was that Napier or Andy? And what had Rachel got to do with it? Was that why she was killed, because she found out and threatened to blow the whistle?'

'Alternatively, Sir, she was setting Napier up again, he found out and bumped her off.'

'OK, but why, in that case, did he put the cash and the gun in his own wardrobe? Did he wish to be arrested?'

'Don't know, Sir.'

'Right. I don't know, either. But one course of action is clear. You take Andy – the egregious Mr Carver – and I'll take Napier, and we'll find out exactly where they were at the probable time of Rachel's murder.'

Spooner called on Andrew Carver the following morning, the eve of the scheduled funeral, and asked his manager to release him from his baking duties for half an hour. They occupied the manager's office, which was neither capacious nor particularly salubrious. Although the smell of cigarette smoke was singularly offensive, Spooner proceeded immediately to the business in hand. It was too cold to open the window, and in any case he thought that would be a discourtesy to the manager.

'Mr Carver,' he said, 'I'm sorry to be troubling you again at this difficult time, but we need to clarify one or two things. Please bear with me.'

Carver said nothing. He sat there in his baker's whites, looking grim and miserable.

'Why didn't you tell us about Rachel's father?' asked Spooner.

'I did. He died when Rachel was five. There's nothing to tell.'

'That's not true, is it? There's everything to tell, and we had to find out by other means. So why did you hide it from us?'

'I didn't hide it from you. It's irrelevant. How could it have anything to do with Rachel's death?'

'I'll tell you why. For a start, the man who killed Len Appleton could well be responsible for shooting Rachel dead. Didn't you think of that? Of course you did, so why not come out with it? Do you want to help us or don't you?'

'Of course I want to help you, but I don't know anything! I've already told you all I know, and Rachel's father doesn't come into it. Rachel went out shopping, she didn't come home, I reported her missing, her body was found. The only person who had any motive to murder Rachel is Napier, but how can I prove he did it?'

'So you know about Napier? How can you possibly know about him?'

Andy realised that he had revealed too much. How easy it is to let information slip out, even with a lifetime of discipline behind one (which was not true of Andy)! He kept silent, wondering how he could now extricate himself from the hole he had dug. Rather than continuing to dig, he decided after a little while to make a clean breast of it: there seemed to be no alternative.

'Sergeant, the whole thing's a mess. Can I tell you the truth?'

'I wish you would.'

'Well, Rachel confided in me that she recognised Napier's voice as belonging to her father's murderer. We heard him talking to a mate of his in a pub six or seven months ago. She became obsessed with putting him away, so she set him up with the raid on the jeweller's shop.'

'You mean you did the dirty work?'

Andy paused, looked shifty and sheepish, and nodded his head.

'Go on.'

'Her next idea was to set him up for an armed robbery, so that he would go down for longer. It all seemed to go according to plan, until something went drastically wrong on Tuesday.'

'What do you think went wrong?'

'Rachel told me that she was going to Napier's house to plant the cash and the gun and then tip the police off.'

'Just a minute: was it a real gun?'

'No, only an imitation.'

'Right, go on.'

'Well, she obviously went to his house, he caught her, shot her and dumped her body. Who else could it have been?'

'How did she intend to get into his house?'

Andy told him about the duplicate key, obtained in the wake of the first attempt on Napier's freedom.

'Well, Mr Carver, I wish you'd told us all this in the beginning. It sheds a completely different light on your wife's murder, you know. But can I just ask you about your own movements on the night your wife went missing? We're going to have to get every detail straight if this case is to stand up in court, whichever way it goes.'

Andrew Carver did not think this the best time to be questioned about his movements: of what relevance could they be? He had nothing to do with it. However, he was sufficiently cowed by his situation as one concealing what could be material evidence that he acceded.

'I came home from work at three, as I usually do. The bakers finish then, and the cleaners take over. Made myself a cup of tea, listened to some music, usual things. Rachel came in a little after four, as she does on a Tuesday. Said she wanted to do some shopping but had forgotten her cheque-book. Told me to meet her at the Happy Haddock at a quarter to six for a fish supper – a little bit of a treat, she said – and disappeared out of the front door. That's the last I saw of her.'

'But you knew she was going to Napier's house at some stage?'

'Yes.'

'And what did you do then?'

'Well, I stayed in, of course, and then went out to meet the wife as arranged.'

'Can anyone vouch for you that you never left the house during that time?'

He thought for a minute.

'Yes, old Mr Jarvis from next door came round to borrow a spanner and stayed an age telling me about his aches and pains: his rheumatic this and arthritic that, or whatever it was. He goes on and on, and I tend to switch off.'

'What time did he come round?'

'Fifteen or twenty minutes after Rachel left.'

'And how long did he stay?'

'Too long. I offered him a cup of tea, and unfortunately he said yes. Must have been half an hour.'

'So that takes us to about five o'clock. What then?'

'How can I remember, Sergeant? I've got other things on my mind.'

'Come on, Mr Carver, it's only three days ago.'

'Gor blimey, what is this, an interrogation?'

'Yes, of sorts. We need to know the movements of everyone involved in this case.'

'After old man Jarvis left – let me think – I cleared away the mugs and sugar-bowl – oh, I know, I then phoned my mate Geoff to fix up a darts match for the weekend. I then had a quick bath before going out.'

'Did anyone see you leave the house?'

More thinking. 'Yes, my other neighbour. She was just coming in from work, and we said hello.'

'Right, Mr Carver, I shall need your mate Geoff's name and address, if you don't mind, and then that'll be all for the moment.'

Meanwhile, the inspector was having a difficult time with Mr Michael Napier. Because the latter had been bailed and was back at work, Wickfield had no choice but to drag him away from his desk while they communed in a private room in Barford Buildings.

'You'll understand, I'm sure, Mr Napier, that we must clarify the movements of everyone connected with this case – Rachel Carver's murder, I mean. I wonder, therefore, whether you'd be good enough to bear with me while we run over the events of Tuesday night.'

'Of course, Inspector. I've nothing to hide.'

Wickfield thought that an odd comment but passed on.

'So, when you left work, what did you do?'

'You do realise I've told you all this once already, do you, Inspector? You can't seriously suspect me of involvement in Mrs Carver's death?'

'Please go on, Mr Napier.'

'I left work as I nearly always do at half-past five. That is, I finish work but take a few minutes to tidy up and collect my coat and so forth. So I left the building at I should think three or four minutes after half-past five. On Tuesdays I meet Justin at the Golden Wheatsheaf – I've told you all this before, Inspector – it's only just round the corner. We stayed about an hour, I should think: we usually do. There are probably plenty of people, apart from the barman, who saw us and remember us. Then I picked my car up at the office and drove home.'

'Would anyone have seen you leave the building?'

'Oh, yes, I should think so. The cleaners are at work by then, for example.'

'And what time did you get home?'

'I don't know exactly. It's only six or seven minutes' drive from town, so I suppose about a quarter to seven.'

'Did you notice anything unusual at home?'

'No, nothing. It was only when the police burst in half an hour later and went through the place as if there were a bomb hidden that I was told about the items in the wardrobe.'

'Can we just go back to Len Appleton's murder in 1951? Rachel Carver seems to have thought you were the murderer, and that's why she was pursuing you.'

'Rachel Carver did? Good heavens, that's news to me, Inspector. Where on earth could she have got that idea from?'

'Well, possibly because she overheard her father call her murderer "Mick" – or at least that's what she told her aunt at the time. You're a Mick, aren't you, Mr Napier?'

'No, there you're wrong, Inspector. I've never been called Mick: Mike, possibly, but usually Michael. No one has ever called me Mick, no one.'

'The police files show that you were interviewed by the police in connexion with Mr Appleton's death, Mr Napier. Do you remember that?'

'Yes, of course I do. But then, you know, I understood that the police spread their net very wide. They took in anyone with the slightest relationship to Mr Appleton, and I happened to be on the very edge of his acquaintance.'

'And presumably you were able to account for your movements satisfactorily to the police at the time?'

'Good heavens, Inspector, I had absolutely nothing to do with the affair. As I say, I was interviewed as a matter of routine and could contribute nothing of any value.'

'How did you know Mr Appleton? You must have known him, otherwise the police wouldn't have interviewed you.'

'My family lived near to theirs when we were young, that's all.'

'Where was this?'

'Look, Inspector, none of this is relevant. It's got absolutely nothing to do with Rachel Carver's death.'

'We'll be judges of that, if you don't mind, Mr Napier. Tell me about your acquaintance with the Appletons.'

'My parents, my brothers and I lived in Worcester at that time. The Appletons lived a few doors down the road. We went to the same school as the three Appleton kids, but not all at the same time. Then they moved away, and we moved away, and that was that.'

'What puzzles me in that case, Mr Napier, is how the police got hold of you in the first place. Why would they be routing around amongst Len Appleton's primary school chums?'

'Can't help you there, Inspector. You'll have to go back to the police notes on the case.'

'Come on, Mr Napier, you must have some idea.'

'As I said, the police were getting desperate and interviewing anyone who had ever had the slightest acquaintance with Mr Appleton or the family. That's what I've always thought.'

'All right, let's not pursue that. It's probably not important anyway. The police also interviewed your brothers.'

'They probably did. I don't remember particularly. This is going back twenty years, you know, and Len's death was on the very edge of our consciousness. Why not ask them, Inspector?'

'I shall, Mr Napier, I shall. Let's come back to the present, then. Someone planted the gun and cash in your house – if you didn't put them there yourself, of course.'

Napier making as if to protest, Wickfield added, 'Only joking, Sir!' and went on, 'The only person other than yourself to have a key is apparently one of your brothers. That's what you told us, I believe.'

'Yes, Inspector, that's quite correct.'

'May I ask where he lives?'

'Noel? Out at Church Lench.'

'Where's that?'

'It's a small village north of here, about five and a half miles, I should think. Very nice church, Inspector, well worth a visit.'

'Yes, thank you, Mr Napier. How often does your brother use his key?'

'Rarely. He doesn't often call when I'm out. Why would he bother?'

'Well, I shall need to speak to him. If he didn't use his key that night, someone else may have borrowed it from him. And what about your other brother?'

'Victor? He lives abroad. Spain. Hardly see him these days.'

'Do you mean there was a row?'

'Well, not exactly. Let's say a difference of opinion.'

'Do Noel and Victor get on?'

'Yes, I think so. In fact I believe Victor was over here staying at his house not so very long ago.'

'How long has he been out in Spain?'

'What has that to do with the price of cheese, Inspector? I don't know: about twenty years, I should say. None of this has anything to do with Mrs Carver's death, has it? If you've finished with your questions, may I get back to work?'

'Yes, I suppose so, Mr Napier, when you've given me the addresses of your two brothers and Mr Blackwater. I admit that at the moment I don't see my way very clearly in this matter, and therefore I cannot afford to leave any stone unturned. I hope you appreciate that. I have no wish to be obstreperous or oppressive, and I apologise if I've given that impression.'

'That's quite all right, Inspector. You have your duty to perform, the same as I have.' With that, he rose and invited Wickfield, with a gesture, to precede him out of the room.

Wickfield and Spooner spent the next few hours, while memories were still reasonably fresh, contacting the witnesses who, they had been assured, could vouch for the movements and innocence of the two chief suspects. All the testimonies seemed satisfactory. Those named as witnesses offered spontaneous corroborations of the statements taken in the interviews. The case against both suspects was weak and the evidence negligible. Firstly, Carver. If he wished to murder his wife, he could do so any time. He need not choose a time of day when people were still about or a place so public as the town shopping-centre. Shooting was risky, because of the noise, and why would he set up Napier in such an obvious and unsubtle way? No one was going to implicate a victim in the eyes of the police in this way. If his plan was to avenge his late and unknown father-in-law by discrediting his murderer, the deduction was that he loved his wife Rachel. None of it made sense. Secondly, Napier. There was no evidence that he was Appleton's killer. On the contrary, he had been investigated at the time and found guiltless. He had a cast-iron alibi for the time of Rachel's murder. No murderer in his right mind would try to conceal the murder weapon, and cash from a raid on the branch of a building society, in so obvious a place as a wardrobe in his own house. There was no evidence he even knew Rachel. His life-style was blameless. Wickfield began to realise that this was not by any means a straightforward case. If Napier and Carver were irrelevant, Wickfield had allowed himself to be sidetracked, and several days had been wasted. On the other hand, he consoled himself with the thought that they could not have avoided conducting the investigation without looking closely into Napier's and Carver's respective roles.

However, two lines of inquiry seemed to suggest themselves. At the station next morning, Wickfield outlined his plan to his assistant.

'Sergeant, I've been mulling over this case and can't see a way forward with the data at our disposal. Have you done any better overnight?'

'No, Sir, I'm afraid to say I haven't.' He sounded as if he thought his failure were directly attributable to a gross lack of intelligence.

'Right, this is what I propose. I have obtained permission from our revered superior – sorry, mustn't be facetious – from Detective Chief Inspector Maxwell, to go to Spain to interview Victor Napier. There's something going on there, but I'm not sure what, and I think a face-to-face talk will do some good. Meanwhile, you are to investigate the Appleton family. We have two members of the same family murdered, at different times and by different methods, it's true, but there must be a connexion. I want you to investigate. For example, Len Appleton may not have been wealthy, but he was by all accounts well-off. His money presumably passed to his daughter. Where is it now? Who would benefit financially from Rachel's death? Again, what happened to the business? Who took it over? Did our colleagues at the time discover any evidence of a family feud? You know the sort of thing, Sergeant. And there's no need to be envious of your inspector living it up on the Costa del Sol. I shall be working – even though, of course, a spot of warmth will be welcome. I'm told daytime temperatures at this time of year are low 60s. Very nice, I must say.'

Seven

*F*rom the aeroplane windows Wickfield looked out through a clear sky to the town of Málaga, as the plane circled the airport before landing. Wickfield had not been to Spain before and knew no Spanish, but he was confident that, for one or two days, he could manage. All he had to do, really, was negotiate an airport. He had arranged with Victor Napier to be picked up at the airport and driven to his home, not far inland from Nerja. As the mountains on their left and the Mediterranean Sea on their right ensured a constantly changing and enticing panorama in the winter sunshine, Wickfield felt no urge to engage in conversation beyond a few introductory remarks on both sides. Covertly he examined his companion as he pretended to admire the mountains. Victor Napier was in his mid to late fifties, Wickfield calculated, and had worn well. He was still youthful in appearance, clean-shaven, with a strong jaw and a masculine nose. His short-cut hair added to the impression of healthy, loose-limbed living. Here was a man at ease with himself, content with his lot. Wickfield looked forward to seeing how he shaped up at interview.

After a drive of thirty or so miles, Napier turned off the main road and took a meandering side-road heading up towards a village on the lower slopes of the Sierra Almijara. The house was a single-storied hacienda with a prominent veranda surrounded by a Mediterranean-style garden. There were a few citrus trees and a few olive trees and some shrubs Wickfield did not recognize. The view out to sea, which he took in as he waited for his host to alight from the car, was glorious, but he knew he could not live here, deeply rooted in the English countryside as he was. Nowhere else would he find the hedgerows and oaks and beeches and ploughed fields of his youth. For the moment, however, he was content to squint into the sun and look out towards Africa.

Victor Napier led the way round to the front of the house and ushered him in. Wickfield could hear the sounds of a piano being played, to his ear very competently. He identified Chopin's barcarolle in F sharp: beautiful! Napier then led the way through a spacious hall-way to the room in which the pianist sat at her instrument. She rose, tall, svelte and elegant, a good few years younger than Napier, Wickfield thought.

'Kimbo, darling, may I introduce Detective Inspector Wickfield from England? Inspector, this is my wife Kimberly, all the way from Hong Kong.'

Introductions made, the two men sat down, while Kimberly, saying she would make coffee, disappeared into the hall.

'Now, Inspector, what can I do for you? Your phone-call said something about Michael being in a spot of trouble and that I might be able to help.'

'Yes, Mr Napier, it's a delicate situation. I understand from your brother that you two don't get on particularly well.'

'No, we don't, not really, but I'm sure that's not relevant to your inquiry. What trouble is Michael in?'

'A few months ago he was sent to prison for robbery. The court really had no alternative, although now it looks much more likely that he was set up. Anyhow, last week more stolen goods, and a gun, were found in his house, and more than that, he is possibly to be arrested on a charge of murder.'

'Murder? Good heavens! Who's he supposed to have murdered?'

'A young woman called Rachel Carver. Does the name mean anything to you?'

'No, not a thing. Should it?'

'Her maiden name was Appleton.' Wickfield waited for the light to dawn.

'Appleton.' Napier ruminated on the name. 'No relation to that chap who got himself murdered way back in the 50s, I suppose?'

'The very same,' Wickfield replied. He was not impressed with Napier's attitude.

'You were at school with him, I believe.'

'Perhaps I was, Inspector, but I really don't remember.'

'But the name does ring a bell?'

'Yes, it does. Didn't he have a couple of sisters? One of them was quite pretty, I seem to recall. But where do I come into the story?'

At that moment, Kimberly reappeared with a tray of coffee and biscuits – 'Home-made almond meringue biscuits, Inspector, in your honour,' she said archly. Putting the tray down, she asked whether the men needed her to stay. Wickfield could see no real harm, but he was unsure how much Napier would care for her to know about his past and his family, so he said gallantly, 'No, no, Mrs Napier, it's really your husband I came to see. And thank you for the biscuits.'

'Now, Mr Napier,' Wickfield said when they were alone again, 'you're going to have to polish up your memory a bit. Len Appleton was killed in February 1951. You were interviewed by the police at the time.'

'Was I? If you say so.'

'This won't do, Mr Napier. I need more cooperation than this, lots more. The alternative is to invite you to Worcester for formal questioning at the station.'

'That's an empty threat, Inspector, and you know it. You can't touch me here: there is no way you can force me to go to Worcester.'

'Well, now, Mr Napier, that may be so, but I'm sure you wouldn't wish your brother to go to gaol for a crime he didn't commit if you could help him out.'

'The point is, I can't help him out. I don't know anything.'

'Well, let's start with Len Appleton. You kept up with him after school, didn't you?' Wickfield was doing some risky guessing, but he was confident that he was doing no more than making sensible deductions from the police record.

'Not really. We all still lived in Worcester, and we bumped into each other occasionally. That's about the sum of it.'

'You knew his wife?'

'Miriam? Certainly did. Would have asked her to marry me myself, if Len hadn't got in first. Lovely girl.' He gazed wistfully out of the window for a moment.

'Did you bear Len a grudge for having beaten you to it?'

'Good Lord, no, Inspector. I've got a gorgeous wife of my own.'

'That's not quite the question I asked you. How long have you been married, may I ask?'

'To Kimbo? Three years. Before that I was married to a harridan who, fortunately for both of us, left.'

'So you could have resented Len's success with Miriam?'

'I could have done, Inspector, but I didn't. Look, where is all this leading?'

'Shall I ask the questions, Mr Napier? Much simpler that way. So you are beginning to remember a little bit now?'

A sullen silence met this sally.

'Let me move on to earlier this week. You were in England, I believe?'

'Was I?' He met Wickfield's steady gaze. 'Yes, sorry, Inspector, I was.'

'You stayed with Noel.'

'Yes. Any reason why I shouldn't?'

'Do you always stay with Noel? Never with Michael?'

'No, I always stay with Noel.'

'What was your row with Michael about?'

'I hated the way he treated his wife and told him so.'

'How did he treat his wife?'

'Like dirt.'

'Is that why they divorced?'

'They didn't divorce, Inspector. She disappeared, and he gave out that she'd left him and that they divorced.'

'When was this?' Wickfield asked sharply.

'Years ago. Can't remember exactly: eight? nine?'

'Please tell me more about it'

'No, I don't think I shall, Inspector, if you don't mind. That would merely be me gossiping. You'd do much better to ask him yourself. After all, my information is just second-hand.'

'OK, let me ask you whether you saw Michael on your latest visit.'

'No, I haven't spoken to him since his wife – "left".'

'How long have you lived in Spain, Mr Napier?'

'I don't know, twenty odd years.'

'Why did you come out here?'

'Look, Inspector, that's my business. I'd love to help, but I can't see what you're getting at.'

'Then let me tell you what I'm getting at. Rachel Carver, née Appleton, was murdered earlier this week. She remembered one thing from her father's murder, which she overheard from the top of the stairs. Her father addressed his killer as "Mick" – but, we think, that could have been Dick, or Nick, or Rick – or' – and this with heavy emphasis – 'Vic.' Wickfield paused. 'Unfortunately we don't know what the row was about. It could have been over a woman.' He paused again, pregnantly. 'Or business, of course. Or almost anything else. That's why the police had to investigate all of Mr Appleton's acquaintances. Now we are working on the hypothesis that Rachel Carver was murdered because she was her father's daughter. Her killer got wind of the fact that she was getting close and chose to put her out of the way rather than wait to be put out of the way himself – or into the way of the police. How's that for a working hypothesis, Mr Napier?'

'Go on. Where do I come in?' was the only reply.

'Let me spell the matter out for you, then. You fled to Spain apparently very shortly after being questioned by the British police in connexion with the murder of Len Appleton. It so happens that you are back in England on a touching visit to your brother Noel when Rachel is murdered. Does that help you to see what I'm getting at?'

'Inspector, you're barking up completely the wrong tree. I didn't "flee" to Spain, as you put it. I came as the result of a long-gestated plan to improve my standard of living. My first wife agreed. Her family knew of our plans. I hoped partly that a change of scene would enable me and Harriet to patch up the marriage. The other part of my hope is neither here nor there. As for my visit to Church Lench this week, I come over once a year to see Noel and his wife, and I stay a week. It's as simple as that. I didn't see Michael, I didn't see Rachel Appleton – Carter, or whatever her name is – I didn't even go to Evesham. Does that satisfy you?'

'Well, I shall ask you to jot down for me before I go where I can get hold of your first wife or her family. But the answer to your question is, No, that doesn't really satisfy me. I want to know the main reason for your coming out to Spain just around the time Len Appleton was killed.'

'There is no mystery about it, as you imply, just embarrassment.'

'I shall not hold an indiscretion against you, Mr Napier. That's not what I'm here for.'

'If you must know, I had a fling – a silly fling – with a young girl at work, and my wife said that we had to move or she would go. As my wife and I were still getting on reasonably well, I reconsidered my position, and we arranged to emigrate. I'm not likely to admit to an affair very readily, am I?'

'OK. Let me ask you now to clarify your movements in England on your latest visit. On what day did you arrive?'

'I generally go and return mid-week, and this time was no exception. Wednesday to Wednesday.'

'How did you spend the time?'

'Oh, dear, Inspector, this is all very tedious. Noel and Shirley both work, so during the day I amuse myself. I went to the Art Gallery in Worcester, window-shopped in Birmingham, had several long walks in the Malverns, that sort of thing. At the weekend, Noel and I played golf, we all three went to the cinema, we had lunch with neighbours on the Sunday. Look, Inspector, I've told you once, I never went near Evesham, I've got nothing to do with any murder or any trouble that Michael has got himself into. I can't help you.'

'Never the less, would you be good enough just to write out for me your exact movements on Tuesday evening?'

'If I have to,' he replied ungraciously. Wickfield waited while his host rose from his chair with ill-concealed temper, searched around for a pen and paper, failed to find any, left the room with a bang, returned a few minutes later, resumed his seat, scratched his chin and finally scribbled a few sentences on his paper. He handed the sheet to Wickfield.

'I hope that keeps you happy, Inspector,' he said with more than a trace of peevishness.

Tuesday afternoon. Lunch in the house, followed by reading the paper, 12.30 to 1.30. Constitutional round the village, 1.30

to 2.00. Read a book 2.00 to around 3.00. Played patience for half an hour or so, then did a few golf swings in the garden. Too cold to stay out long, so switched on the television. Shirley came home at 5.15 and we had a cup of tea together in the kitchen. Noel came in at 5.45 and we sat chatting, the three of us. Supper at around 7.00. Then we played canasta through the evening.

'Thank you, Mr Napier, I'm sure that will do admirably. I have one final question for you: how was Michael's name shortened by those who knew him well?'

'Mike. Our parents called him Michael, but everyone else Mike. Why?'

'Did anyone ever call him "Mick"?' persisted Wickfield, ignoring Victor's counter-question.

'No, never in my hearing. May be different now, of course, I wouldn't know.'

Since there was no flight back to Birmingham until the following morning, Wickfield prevailed on Napier to drive him back to Málaga, where he found a small hotel sufficient for his needs. Napier, to do him justice, did offer a bed for the night, but the inspector thought that relations were too strained to make a longer stay at the Napier homestead comfortable, either for him or for them, however much he would have liked to see more of the seductive Kimberly. As he sat over his bacalao and sangria, he ruminated on the interview. Had he learnt much? Napier – Victor, that is – had implied that Michael's wife's departure was not all that it was given out to be. On the other hand, knowing that the police were anxious to trace a 'Mick', he had cleared his brother of ever being known as 'Mick'. What he bestowed with one hand, therefore, he retracted with the other. As a whole, the interview had left an unsavoury taste in his mouth. He was unsure whether he could believe Napier's – Victor's – protestations of innocence. If he were guilty of two murders, he would naturally prevaricate. Would he not, however, prevaricate more suavely, less indignantly? He would surely not wish to antagonize the investigating detective. Although Wickfield was puzzled and dissatisfied, he knew that nothing was to be gained for the moment in remaining in Spain, and he therefore determined to pursue his inquiries in Britain with as much grace and enthusiasm as he could muster.

When he met Spooner the following afternoon, he asked him how his own inquiries had fared.

'Well, Sir, I had a busy - and I must say enjoyable - day, and I've been trying to put it all together for you this morning. The trouble is, I'm not sure it yields much useful information.'

'Don't worry, Sergeant, a single crumb of useful information would satisfy me hugely at the moment. Let me have what you've got.'

'OK, Sir, here we go. I went back as far as Len Appleton's grandfather, John, who founded the firm in 1896.'

Spooner was consulting a note-book with a spiral binding in which he had scribbled notes with arrows at various points to guide him in the coherent imparting to Wickfield of the information he had gathered from a number of sources.

'The family was well-to-do even then,' he began, 'but John, being the third son, had little prospect of inheriting a great fortune and knew he would have to depend largely on his own efforts. He borrowed a small sum of money off his grandmother – who was his grandfather's cousin as well as wife - and set up in the business of importing raw rubber and then turning it into products for industry – whatever his clients demanded. When he died in 1921, at the relatively early age of fifty-six, his eldest son Jonas took over the business. He'd been brought up to it and knew it from the bottom up. He made sure that the fiftieth anniversary was celebrated in style and splashed over the *Worcestershire Sketch*. That's where a lot of my information comes from. Funnily enough, he also married his cousin, Ethel, and they had three children. The eldest was our Leonard, born in 1916 and destined to continue his grandfather's firm, which, when his father died in 1948, he did. However, Len's priorities differed in one important respect from those of his forebears: making money was not his main aim in life. In the *Who's Who of Worcestershire* of 1950, his interests are listed as sailing, botany, sport and shooting. In 1948, Merton College, Oxford, let him the exclusive right of shooting and killing game on an estate at Bielby, in east Warwickshire, for an annual rent of twenty guineas. Leonard agreed to pay all rates and parochial assessments that might be levied in respect of the shooting, while the college agreed to keep the plantations on the estate properly fenced from trespass by livestock. In the same *Who's Who*, a footnote reads: 'The Family has been engaged in the importation of rubber for four generations' – a slight exaggeration. The *Worcester Gazette* of 3 November 1950 referred to Leonard as "one of the city's most highly regarded businessmen".

'I've said that making money was not top of Leonard's list of priorities. It seems that Low Church Anglicanism substituted for Mammon, and he had a reputation amongst who knew him best for integrity and diffidence. He supported a wide range of charities in the city. In due course, when he was twenty-nine and still learning the business, he married a young woman called Miriam Hodgson, who was known locally as Miss Beautiful Worcester. On his marriage, Leonard moved out of the family home and bought Ditcham Lodge on the edge of Evesham, which is where he met his death.

'Now Leonard had two younger sisters, Claire, born in 1918, and Sarah, born in 1920. Both married. Claire married a college sweetheart called Edwin Jones, who turned out to be a bit of a wastrel. They live somewhere to the north-west of the city. Sarah we've met. In 1942 she married Bernard Young, a solicitor, and as you know they live at Hampton. Their family consists of a son James and a daughter Louise, both away from home and married. Although Sarah is four years Leonard's junior, she married much younger than he did, and her family are correspondingly older than poor Rachel. As far as I can gather, Claire and Sarah never really got on, and they don't see much of each other now. Claire's two boys, Sam and George, have nothing to do with their aunt, although I don't think there's anything sinister in this, not from our point of view.

'When Len died, he left no will. Letters of administration were given to Sarah and a solicitor from outside the family, a partner in the long-standing firm of Mowbray, Mowbray, Son and Mowbray, of Worcester. The trust specified that Rachel was to inherit on her twenty-first birthday, which fell on 3 September 1966. As far as the firm was concerned, three of the directors bought the Appleton family out, and the purchase price was added to Len's estate. I went to see the solicitor and had a talk with him. He was willing to open up, in view of Rachel's death. Apparently Rachel inherited her father's financial circumspection or lack of ambition or whatever one wishes to call it; she also learnt from her father's death to make provision in the case of untimely decease. She bought the house she and Andy moved into on their marriage, and then invested the rest of her trust money in a trust for her own children, with the proviso that if she died childless, the monies were to go in equal shares to her husband and Sarah's children, James and Louise, whom she regarded as her siblings. The house was to go unencumbered to Andrew.

'The police inquiry at the time of Leonard's death uncovered no rivals for control of the firm, no competitors anxious to force him out of business, no enemies intent on his destruction. That doesn't mean to say there weren't any, of course, but our colleagues seem to have been pretty thorough. They were probably motivated in part by the fact that the midnight strangulation of Mr Appleton, who was both a prominent citizen and a young murder victim, was a *cause célèbre*. Len's books contained the names of many industrialists who used his products. He provided components for the armed forces, manufacturers of agricultural machinery, the automobile industry, the aircraft industry and so on, but there was no skulduggery that the police could fix on which could provide any sort of motive for murder. The buy-out on the part of the directors was thoroughly investigated, but it was proved beyond doubt that the action was contemplated only in the aftermath of Leonard's death and could not have formed the basis of a murder plot. Furthermore, the three directors concerned were as virtuous as their leader. It was really no surprise that our colleagues failed to identify the murderer: there were just no suspects. The Napier brothers did not feature in any list of friends in Appleton's possession, and their inclusion in the police trawl was more an admission of failure in other areas of the investigation than part of a strategy expected to yield results. So as I say, Sir, not very productive.'

'Oh, I wouldn't say that, Sergeant. We might well spot something interesting when we've had a bit of time to mull over it. In any case, it had to be done, didn't it?'

'And how did you get on, Sir?' Spooner asked.

After an account of his trip to Spain, Wickfield told his assistant that two necessities that arose from his visit to Mr and Mrs Victor Appleton were an interview with the third Napier brother on the one hand and an interview with Victor's first wife on the other. He admitted that neither promised to be rich in information, but, in the absence of any sort of progress in the case, they could not make matters any obscurer - could they? First of all, however, they had to investigate the fate of Michael's wife.

Eight

Before any action in that direction could be taken, however, Wickfield had an unexpected telephone call. The apparatus on his desk rang, to his imagination more imperiously than usual, and the station receptionist told him that a Reverend Giles Sercombe wished to speak with him.

'Put him on!'

'Inspector, I'm sorry I didn't catch your surname from the receptionist, but I understand you're in charge of the investigation into Rachel Carver's murder.'

'I am. May I ask who you are? I mean, I know you're a reverend, but are you from Evesham?'

'Yes, Inspector. I'm the minister at St Mark's Baptist chapel.'

'Ah!' Wickfield said, enlightened.

'Look,' the minister said, 'I'd very much appreciate it if next time you're this way you could drop in to see me. Or I could come up to Worcester. I think I need to tell you something.'

'You think you need to tell me something. Well, that sounds intriguing, Reverend. My sergeant and I can easily come over this morning, if that's convenient. What do you think?'

'That would suit splendidly. Monday's the quietest day of the week, and I shall be at home. Do you know where we are?'

'Next to the church?' Wickfield hazarded.

'Well, actually three doors down, No.16. I hope to see you shortly. Thank you so much.'

Wickfield and Spooner drove down to Evesham yet again. It was a fine January morning. A light breeze rustled the bare trees in the station compound, and although the men heard a great tit giving forth exuberantly, they did not succeed in spotting him. Spooner covered the fifteen miles with commendable caution and road-sense, despite which they were nearly involved in an accident as they negotiated Pershore when a lorry decided to indicate left and then turn right. The policemen arrived at the Sercombe residence – an unpretentious town-house - were warmly received and, after the making of introductions and the hanging of coats in the hall, were ushered into a small lounge at the front of the house.

'Very good of you to come, Inspector, Sergeant. If the neighbours have recognised policemen arriving, it will seem perfectly natural for you to call, in the circumstances, and tongues won't wag – no more than usual, anyway! Sit down, make yourselves comfortable. I'll soon have a pot of tea for you.'

The Reverend Sercombe was an immensely tall and stooped individual, with sparse, gingery hair and thick spectacles. His face radiated intelligence and benevolence in equal measure, although he might also have been slightly dotty. He re-appeared with a tray of tea and biscuits.

'My wife would have made a much better job of this, Gentlemen, but she's at work. She'll be sorry to have missed you – not that she knows anything about the business on which I have called you today.'

After some preliminary courtesies demanded by the occasion, Sercombe cleared his throat, as if preparatory to launching into speech, and then fell silent. He coughed. He fidgeted. Eventually, however, he managed to begin.

'Gentlemen,' he said, 'I've debated within myself whether to speak to you at all. I mean, all citizens are called on to assist the police, and the fact that poor Mrs Carver's body was found in my chapel grounds gives me every excuse to contact you, but none the less I feel very awkward. I'm still not sure whether I should be saying anything at all. You'll appreciate my indecision when I've finished.'

He worked his heavy spectacles back up the bridge of his nose and mopped his brow with a large handkerchief. He seemed relieved to have reached this point in his discourse but in need of further inner courage to proceed.

'I know from – er, well, from gossip – no, let me rephrase that, Gentlemen: it has come to my ears that you have interviewed Mr Michael Napier in connexion with Mrs Carver's death, and it is of him that I wish to speak.'

Surely nothing could justify such embarrassment? Wickfield and Spooner waited patiently.

'Michael has been a member of my flock ever since I came here, nearly fifteen years ago now. Before that I was a minister in the north of England – a barren but somehow homely sort of place; vast expanses of moorland, harsh winds off the North Sea, snow-drifts in winter: getting about was very difficult, you know, but a very warm people. You've probably been there, even if only driving through. Some very attractive little towns, you know. Hexham, for example. Such a lovely abbey church. And Rothbury: delightful small shopping centre, unspoilt – as yet – by the big national emporia. And then there's Alnwick Castle: a magnificent pile. But where was I? Oh, yes, sorry, *revenons à nos moutons*, as – oh, dear, I've forgotten who said that. Not Voltaire, was it? Bossuet? Anyway, it doesn't matter. Michael Napier. A fine, upstanding chap. A regular member of the congregation here. Sings in the choir. The choir rehearses on a Sunday morning, then sings at the service. It's so difficult these days to get people to come in during the week – they've always got something else on, you know – so we decided to have a forty-five minute practice before worship on a Sunday, and that's been much more successful. They don't tackle the supreme heights of the repertoire, you understand: fairly straightforward stuff, just to raise worship above the level of the aesthetically pedestrian and banal. We're very lucky to have the head of music at Evesham High School amongst our number, and he does sterling work in coaching the choir.'

'You were saying about Michael Napier, Minister,' Wickfield prompted, anxious both not to antagonize their informant – if such he ever turned out to be – and yet to coax him into divulging whatever was on his mind.

'Yes, yes, of course. Do forgive me. I'm a wanderer, I'm afraid. My wife's always correcting me. Right, to the point. Well, you will realise that the discovery of a murder victim in my church-grounds has been very unsettling. You see, I told myself at first that the murderer chose a random spot in which to dump – seems such an unpleasant word – to dump the body. Then I thought, to my horror, that perhaps it was a member of my own congregation. After all, how many other Evesham citizens are aware of the piece of ground behind the chapel, tucked away as we are in a small cul-de-sac in what is not exactly the town's busiest street? I wager that not even all my congregation know of it – or at least have focused on it. Now a man – or woman, I suppose, but I don't wish to teach you your business, Gentlemen – in the position of our murderer would not wish to delay disposing of the corpse, and he would naturally choose a discreet place already familiar to him. The murderer's not going to wish to spend a lot of time hunting round for a suitable spot if he can help it. You see, I reasoned that Mrs Carver would not have been shot on the spot – much too noisy. Although the people at the back of the church premises can't see over the hedge that divides our land from their gardens, they would hear readily enough if there were a gun-shot. So I thought that perhaps one of my own congregation knew something about it. But I should have thought before, Inspector: you haven't caught the murderer, have you? If you have, what I'm saying is all so much waste of breath, and a possible cause of scandal to boot.'

'No, Mr Sercombe, we've not caught him – or her – yet, I'm afraid. Please continue with your story.'

'Well, I ran over all the parishioners in my mind's eye. I didn't do it formally, you understand: no working systematically through the list of covenanted givers, nothing like that. No, I just reviewed my flock in my head, as it were.'

The Reverend Giles Sercombe paused once again to adjust his spectacles, to take a drink of his rapidly cooling tea and to help himself to a biscuit. (He'd dug out a packet of digestives reserved, he told us, and when necessary renewed, for just such an occasion.) Having given himself a small breathing-space, and offered his visitors another draught from the pot, he resumed his narrative – if such a disjointed statement could be called a narrative.

'As I went over the parishioners, visualizing them in my mind, Michael Napier kept drawing himself to my attention. I phrase it like that because that's how it seemed to me at the time: I wasn't thinking actively of him more than of the other members of the church – old Mrs Watkins, for example – I dismissed her straightaway because she can hardly walk, poor dear, and even when she does, she uses one of those frame things for support, otherwise, I suppose, she'd just topple over at the first sign of a bump in the pavement -- or, just to illustrate to you that I was quite impartial in my review, young Mr Whipple, who is a staunch leader of the Youth Group and a really nice chap -- you couldn't really meet a nicer chap anywhere -- so good with the young people, happily married with two young children of his own, a real example of Christian living - or Nigel Dedham, you know, the farmer from out at, oh, what's the name of his place, again? But no, I forgot, you're not from round here. Oh, dear, I fear I've wandered again. Where was I? Yes, yes, Michael Napier. Now I asked myself why he should be forcing himself on my attention. Did I mention that that's how it seemed to me at the time?'

Wickfield and Spooner nodded in unison.

'I did? Sorry, I'm not very good at coming to the point, am I? I'm not usually like this, I can assure you. Must be because it's Monday.'

Wickfield could not see the relevance of Monday, and he forgave himself for failing to agree with Mr Sercombe on his wider self-description and for wondering irreverently what on earth his sermons were like. An hour's oratory would not suffice to bring forth a single application of the Gospel to present-day living. On the other hand, one could not possibly dislike the man: a genuine minister of the Gospel, a kindly pastor to his flock, and no doubt an exemplary husband and father.

'Nine years ago, Michael Napier's wife left him. At least, that's the story he gave out. There was no publicity, no scandal, no gossip that I ever heard. Sorry, there we are back to gossip, again. I hope you don't get the impression, Gentlemen, that I spend my time listening to small-town tittle-tattle. I can assure you I don't, but then if I closed my ears to everything I'm told, I could well miss out on who's in trouble, who needs a helping hand in illness or family bereavement or the loss of a job and so on. I can't go around pretending that I live in a monastery, can I? Well, I heard that Michael Napier's wife had left him, and I went round to see him, on the pretext of asking him about how he thought young Graham Speed was shaping up as the new choir-master. He's the teacher from the High School I mentioned before. I did mention him before, did I?'

Both his guests nodded in agreement. This was very trying, but neither wished to be impolite: gentlemen both, by upbringing and by inclination.

'He seemed pleased to see me, and in due course he told me all about his happy marriage, and how he couldn't understand why his wife had left him, and how her note of departure gave no real clue to her motives, and so on. He seemed, as of course he would, perfectly genuine. He had apparently come home from work one day to find a scribbled note on the kitchen table saying that she had gone, that he was not to try to find her, that she was sorry if she caused him pain but she couldn't go on as she was. And that was it. I listened sympathetically, and thereafter nothing more about it was said between us.'

None of this seemed very startling, and Wickfield began to wonder whether their visit in response to Mr Sercombe's summons was to prove a damp squib. The minister resumed his narrative.

'However, about six months ago I had a visit from Mrs Carver.'

Wickfield interrupted the minister in his surprise at this piece of intelligence.

'Did you know her previously, Mr Sercombe?'

'No, not at all. I'd had never seen her before, to the best of my knowledge, and she certainly did not attend our church. As I say, she called one day, and we had a long conversation. The difficulty is that she swore me to secrecy, and I have turned over and over in my mind whether her death releases me from my promise of secrecy or not. I have eventually decided, after due prayer and reflexion, that it does. On the other hand, what she told me is not for public hearing, and I trust that it goes no further than these four walls except, Gentlemen, with the utmost discretion. I know I can rely on your discretion.'

He looked first at Wickfield, then at Spooner, but he said nothing further for a moment. They did not speak either but merely nodded sagely.

'First of all, she told me that she was convinced that Michael Napier had been responsible for her father's death in 1951. I questioned her closely, of course, but I was not in a position to challenge her account of the affair – or at least as much of it as she had been able to piece together over the years, which was not much. At that stage, her accusation was mere suspicion, as far as I was concerned, and I wondered whether there was more to come. She then told me that she had determined on revenge. I immediately remonstrated with her, as was my duty. "Revenge belongs to God," I told her. "He will repay." I talked quite a bit, I remember, about leaving matters in God's hands, as the Bible dictates.'

Wickfield had no difficulty in imagining the minister waxing tedious on the Bible's teaching on revenge. It was a wonder that the poor girl did not immediately leave the house, business unfinished. However, she seemed not to have done so.

'She brushed all that aside,' the minister continued. '"The point is this," she said. "I know for a fact that he murdered his wife, and I want to use that information to get him locked up for good as a punishment." "I see," I responded as non-committally as I could. "If you know that for a fact, it is your duty to go to the police." I told her this without prevarication. You agree with me, of course, Gentlemen? She had a duty to go to the police. That was absolutely clear, and I told her so. I made no bones about it. "It is your duty to go to the police," I said. "Unfortunately," she replied, "I can't do that. You see, Minister, they wouldn't take any notice of me. I'm nobody. I've got no proof, but if you went to the police, they'd take notice of you. After all, you're his minister." "Yes, I am," I said, "but that doesn't give me any right to go to the police with mere supposition. You wouldn't want me to get him into bad odour with the police on the basis of mere surmise, would you?" "But it's not mere surmise, Minister. I know what happened, only I haven't got the evidence to prove it." "Have you any evidence at all?" I asked her. You see, I didn't wish her to go away feeling that I hadn't given her a fair hearing or that I wasn't taking her seriously. She was only a young woman, obviously deeply troubled, and I was determined to help her if I could. The Bible tells us to turn a friendly countenance to those in need, as you well know, Gentlemen. So I asked her -- or am I repeating myself? -- whether she had any support for her story at all. "Oh, yes," she replied, "I know exactly what happened." "So what did happen?" I naturally asked. It seemed the obvious thing to say. After all, if she had a case, I might well have gone to the police on her behalf, as she requested.'

'And what did she say?' Wickfield inquired, hoping that his impatience was not betraying itself.

'This is what she told me, Inspector, but I must stress again that it was confidential and that I'm telling you only because she's dead and it may have a bearing on your present case.'

'Yes, quite, Mr Sercombe, we appreciate your concern.'

'Well, when she was trying to find out about Mr Napier – because she thought he was her father's killer, you understand – she knocked one day on the door of his neighbour – a Mrs Hailebury-Smithers – and was invited in. The old dear was lonely, I suppose. Anyway, this Mrs Hailebury-Smithers told Rachel, apparently, that the day before Mrs Napier – Trudy – was supposed to have quitted the marital homestead, she saw Mr and Mrs Napier leave the house in the car as if going out for the evening. Neither had any luggage. Trudy had a handbag, as you'd expect. It was well after midnight when the Napier car returned – with only one occupant. It was the following day that Michael Napier gave out that he found the note from his wife when he got back from work. That has to be a lie, because, you see, Inspector, Sergeant, Trudy hadn't been in the house to leave it. What this Mrs Hailebury-Smithers deduced was that Michael Napier, whom she disliked, apparently – said he gave her the creeps, or words to that effect – took his wife into the country, strangled her so that there was no blood on his clothes or in his car, got rid of the body, in a flooded quarry or down a disused mineshaft – the countryside may be shrinking, Gentlemen, but there are still plenty of places to hide a body if you're determined enough, or perhaps if you walk a lot and take note of what's about you – now, where was I? Oh, yes. Having disposed of the body, Napier returns home as if all were well and leaves for work as usual on the following morning. Rachel asked Mrs H-S why Michael Napier should wish to murder his wife. "He treated her like dirt, dear, always did, but of course I don't know what got into his head to murder her at that particular time." Rachel then asked her why she hadn't gone straight to the police. "The police?" expostulated Mrs H-S – although thinking back to our conversation, I don't think Rachel can have used the word "expostulated" – not quite an everyday word, is it? A pity – "What could I have told them? They would just have said that I was mistaken in not seeing Trudy return home that night with her husband. And the fact that she wasn't seen leaving the house the following day – I'm presuming that none of the neighbours saw her: they couldn't have done, could they, if she was murdered the night before? – is not evidence: a mere negative can't be evidence, can it, dear? They'd have dismissed me as a busybody. In any case, dear" – and here, according to Rachel, she lowered her voice to a whisper – "if Napier found out that I had gone to the police, my life wouldn't have been worth tuppence. No, no, I preferred to say nothing and be safe."'

'There are still aspects of the business I don't understand,' said Wickfield. 'Did nobody report Mrs Napier missing? Her family? Her work? Was there no investigation at all?'

'That was exactly the question I put to Rachel, Inspector. "Did nobody report Mrs Napier missing?' I asked. Trudy had no family, or none to speak of, and Mrs Hailebury-Smithers presumed that Napier had given out to Trudy's work-place the same story he had concocted for the neighbours. She added – and this was news to me, I admit – that Napier didn't treat his wife well and that the surprise was that she hadn't left him before.'

'And what about this Mrs Hailebury-Smithers? Can't she be persuaded to go to the police now?'

'Oh, no, Inspector, she's dead. Rachel had been back to see her, a few weeks after her original conversation, to have another go at persuading her to come forward, and another neighbour told her that she had died in hospital and that the house was shortly to be put up for sale. So Rachel was left with a suspicion and no eye-witness. The police would not have acted on her story. That's why she came to see me.'

'And do you believe her story?' This was Spooner.

'Well, Sergeant, let's put it this way. If Michael Napier murdered Rachel's father, and if he murdered his wife – big ifs, of course – he would be quite capable of murdering Rachel, wouldn't he? As I say, after much thought and prayer, I decided that I owed Rachel at least this, to speak to you in confidence and pass on her concerns.'

'Yes, thank you, Mr Sercombe,' said Wickfield, 'you did the right thing, and we appreciate your discretion. In case you're uneasy in your mind at sowing suspicion about a member of your congregation, I must tell you that at the moment we don't think Mr Napier can have had anything to do with the deaths of Rachel or Rachel's father. You see, according to Rachel, the murdered man called his aggressor Mick, and Mr Napier has never been known as Mick; and he has a cast-iron alibi for the time of Rachel's death. You were quite right, however, to contact us, and we may yet find what you have told us has a direct bearing on Rachel's death. So, many thanks, and for the moment don't think too harshly of Mr Napier, will you? He could be perfectly innocent.'

Nine

*A*fter their conversation with the Reverend Giles Sercombe, which had answered, at least partially, one of their pressing questions, Wickfield split the remaining two tasks between him and his assistant. He thought he would interview Mr Noel Napier himself, while Spooner talked to Victor's first wife.

Church Lench, home to Shirley and Noel Napier, is, as Wickfield discovered, situated in a charming and unspoilt rural area of east Worcestershire, one of a group of small villages and hamlets with the suffix Lench (Abbot's Lench, Rous Lench, Atch Lench, Sheriff's Lench ...). (He presumed that Lench was a family name; or perhaps the family was named after the villages?) As he drove out on a cold, clear January afternoon, he marvelled at the countryside's ability to scintillate and incandesce, even in winter, despite human attempts to destroy it with ugly towns and uglier factories: the industrial estates, the housing estates, the ever-spreading suburbs, electricity pylons and telegraph poles, advertisement hoardings, ever more roads. The Napiers occupied a large, detached residence in the middle of the village, with views to the church one side and to open countryside on the other: woods and ploughed fields and trimmed hedgerows and flocks of wheeling birds. The exterior said 'money', in large quantities. Wickfield wondered what the Napiers did for a living in order to afford such style. He parked in the street and advanced with appropriate diffidence through the wrought-iron gate to the handsome front-door. A well-groomed woman of fifty answered his ring and, assuring him that her husband would be home any minute, guided him into a large and opulent sitting-room. The carpet featured leaves and flower-heads scattered on a beige background. In the corner of the room stood a baby grand piano, surmounted by a bowl of cut flowers and a family photograph in a gilt frame. Heavy, light-gold curtains hung by the full-length windows. The furniture consisted of a luxurious chaise-longue, some occasional tables and a random collection of antique armchairs, tastefully dotted round the room to provide enough accommodation but not to clutter the room's admirable proportions. A spaniel sleeping in front of the hearth ignored him. Wickfield's hostess and he had no difficulty in engaging in conversation as they waited for the man of the house to return from his day's labours.

Noel Napier was a tall and broad man in his mid-fifties, in a bespoke suit of pin-striped blue. Wickfield had no difficulty in visualising him as the eldest of the three brothers. Napier's large hand grasped Wickfield's in a warm gesture of welcome, and the three of them sat down to a pot of tea thoughtfully provided by Mrs Napier.

'We are privileged to welcome a Detective Inspector in our midst,' Noel observed – to Wickfield's annoyance. 'To what do we owe this pleasure, Inspector?'

His wife answered in Wickfield's stead. 'The inspector has called in connexion with a murder inquiry, haven't you, Inspector?' She turned winsomely in his direction.

'Mr and Mrs Napier, my business is soon stated and soon dealt with. As you say, Mrs Napier, I have called in connexion with the death of a Mrs Rachel Carver in Evesham, on Tuesday of last week. As part of that inquiry, I had occasion to interview your brother Michael: the dead girl had apparently planted some incriminating evidence in his house. I should perhaps explain also that we think Rachel's death may be connected with that of her father in 1951, on which occasion you were interviewed, Mr Napier, as one who had been at school with Leonard Appleton, the murdered man. Now we are just running over the two cases together to see whether we can pick out any useful leads.'

'Yes, Inspector,' Mr Napier said in polite acknowledgement.

'Now police questioning at the original inquiry centred on acquaintances of the deceased whose forenames ended in –ic(k), namely Dick, Mick, Nick, Rick and Vic, and – please don't take this amiss, Sir – your brothers Michael and Victor were naturally included, as you may remember. We think that Rachel may have been murdered to prevent her revealing any more about her father's murderer, and we have therefore had to ask both Michael and Victor for details of their whereabouts last Tuesday afternoon, at the time of Rachel's death. Would you be kind enough' – and Wickfield's glance took in both his hosts – 'to confirm what Victor told me when I saw him in Spain a few days ago?'

'And what *did* he tell you?' Shirley inquired.

'Well, if you can tell me what you three did that afternoon, I shall be able to confirm his account - or not, of course, as the case may be.'

'Let me go and fetch the diary, Inspector,' Mrs Napier said. 'That would be a good start, I should think.' She stood up and left the room with grace, returning shortly with a red, leather-bound diary of engagements.

After leafing back a week, she announced that there was no entry for that day other than that Victor was staying with them.

'Now, Noel,' she said, 'what do you imagine we did last Tuesday? Any ideas?'

'Well, dear, you would have got home at around a quarter past five, as usual, and I would have followed you a bit later. I suppose we had our usual supper at seven, after a snifter, and then we probably played cards for the evening. Am I right, do you think?'

'Yes, I should think so, dear. Does that fit with your findings, Inspector?' She turned a broad smile on Wickfield. The unworthy suspicion that Victor had fed his brother and sister-in-law a line to confound the dim inspector crossed his suspicious mind.

'Yes, that's exactly the information I've got, Mrs Napier. But do you know what Victor was doing before you got home?'

'Well, not exactly, of course, but I think he told me he'd been watching a spot of television.' Was this too pat or the naked truth?

'Could I ask you a question on a different subject, while I'm here? It concerns Michael's wife. What happened to her?'

He saw his hosts exchange glances. As Mrs Napier made no attempt to open her mouth, speech was left to her husband.

'About eight or nine years ago,' he said, 'she left him unexpectedly. I've no idea what has happened to her since.'

'Did they get on? I mean, at all?'

'Oh, yes, they were married for ten or eleven years, seemingly happily.'

'So what happened?'

'As I say, Inspector, she left a note one day to say she wouldn't be back, and Michael found it when he returned home that evening. As far as we know, he's never seen her since.'

'Was there anything suspicious about her departure?'

Wickfield detected another exchange of glances between Napier and his wife.

'No, Inspector,' Napier said. 'Why, do you think there might be?'

'No why, really. Tell me, did you two get on with her?'

'Yes,' Mrs Napier answered immediately. 'I liked her very much. She was a sensible, down-to-earth sort of woman, with a good sense of humour and plenty about her.'

'Why do you think they divorced?'

'They've never divorced, that I know of,' said Napier. 'No, it was simply that they weren't really suited, and it took them ten years to discover that fact.'

'Victor tells me that he and Michael don't get on. Do you know why that is?'

'Well, Inspector, I am breaking no confidences if I tell you that Victor thought Michael didn't treat Trudy well and told him so. Michael exploded, and they've never really talked since. That's about the size of it.'

'Well, that's all very helpful. Now again to another matter: I understand from Michael that you have a key to his house. Is that correct?'

'Yes, perfectly, Inspector. We exchanged keys years ago; seemed a sensible precaution in case of emergencies.'

'Did your daughters ever use it?'

'Hardly ever, I should say. They went down only if Michael were expecting them.'

'Is it possible that the key was ever used by somebody else?'

'No, I think we can exclude that. You're thinking about someone planting evidence on Michael? Impossible, I should say. What do you think, Shirley?'

'Quite agree. I wish we could help you with Michael's troubles, Inspector, but we really don't know anything.'

'Well, thank you, Mr and Mrs Napier, for your time. I trust I shan't need to bother you again.'

Wickfield was thoughtful as he was shown to the front-door, walked down the front path and drove off into the darkness.

Meanwhile his assistant, Detective Sergeant Spooner, was wrestling, metaphorically speaking, with Harriet Cosgrove, formerly Harriet Napier, divorced wife of Victor. Mrs Cosgrove and her husband Eamonn lived in Droitwich, in a cul-de-sac of the type of modern house known, for some obscure reason, as 'executive'. Mrs Cosgrove had been invited to be at home for the sergeant's visit. He apologised for having to trouble her and assured her that his business would not take long. She was one of the first people in his experience to check his identity, which satisfied him that he was dealing with a person who could command his respect – if that were a consideration. She was a plump fifty, her hair tied back in a rough pony-tail, house-slippers on her feet, a sort of house-coat round her body.

'Now, Sergeant,' she began with brusque efficiency, 'you told me this was to do with last week's murder of a Mrs Rachel Carver in Evesham. First of all, I don't know a Rachel Carver, and secondly, I haven't been to Evesham for years. So what's it all about?'

'Mrs Cosgrove, Rachel Carver's maiden name was Appleton. Her father was Leonard Appleton.'

'Ah!' she said. 'You're not raking all that up again, are you?'

'The truth is, we think the two deaths may be connected. Or let us say that one hypothesis is that whoever murdered Mr Appleton also murdered his daughter. Now you will doubtless remember that your first husband Victor and his two brothers were all questioned by the police at the time – '

'Yes, but only because they had been at primary school with Len – I ask you!'

' – and we're just running over that original inquiry again to see whether anything the police discovered at the time makes more sense now in the light of the present death. So please bear with me if I ask you to go over what you remember of the original death.'

'Well, what do you want to know?'

'Were you already married to Victor at the time?'

'No, engaged.'

'Did you know his two brothers?'

'Yes, but not very well.'

'Do you remember the police coming round?'

'I remember Victor telling me he'd been interviewed. I also remember he told me what a waste of time it was, because he couldn't tell the police anything at all about Len's murder. Why should he? He hardly knew him.'

'But he did know him?'

'Yes, he knew him. In fact, he was going to approach him for a loan for a business venture, but Len died before anything came of it. That's why we moved to Spain – Victor thought it would be cheaper over there. If Len had lived, our lives might have been very different.'

'What I don't understand, Mrs Cosgrove, is why your husband would go to Len for a loan if he hardly knew him.'

'That's easy, Sergeant. Victor had tried everywhere else, and in any case Len was known to be loaded. Vic was just trying to use their primary school days together as a lever. It was a nice try, but it didn't come off. So we emigrated.'

'I see. Did you know Len?'

'Yes, and I don't mind your knowing that I took a shine to him and hoped he'd propose. Instead he set his heart on that lovely looking Miriam Cantucci, the one they called Miss Beautiful Worcester. I picked up Victor a year or two later, when it became as clear as daylight that my hopes were to be dashed for ever, but I suppose we weren't really suited; perhaps I wasn't ready for another love. Pity, really. Anyhow, I'm happy now.'

'Tell me about the two brothers, Mrs Cosgrove. Can you see either of them in the role of murderer?'

'Ooh, that's a straight question, if ever there was one! Noel was the eldest of the three: an ambitious, cocky sort of chap, who was going to make money whatever he turned his hand to.'

'And what did he turn his hand to?'

'Went to university, did our Noel, read mathematics and became

84

an actuary. Haven't seen him since Vic and I split up, but he was doing all right then, I can tell you.'

'Would he have any grievance against Len? Do you know of any quarrel between them?'

'No. I don't think they kept up after school. Vic told me that Noel was as surprised as he was to get a visit from the police.'

'And what about Michael?'

'Ah, now Michael's a different matter – bit of a dark horse. But there again, Sergeant, I haven't seen Michael for years.'

'But what was he like as a young man? You would have known him in his early or mid-thirties.'

'Yes, he was a couple of years older than my Victor, and I immediately took to the man. He wasn't easy to get to know, and I confess I never succeeded, but he had charm - and presence. He was already married when I met Victor, and I remember being invited a number of times to their house. I took an immediate dislike to Trudy – little more than a fishwife. How he put up with her I'll never know.'

'She left him eventually, didn't she?'

'Yes, but we were living in Spain at the time, so I never knew exactly what happened, but yes, she left him. I felt so sorry for Michael, because he'd done his very best for her, as far as I could see. Nothing was ever good enough for her, and she had a shrewish temper. Victor liked her -- but then anything busty in a skirt was his idea of heaven – but Noel loathed her.'

Since no more was possible that evening, Wickfield decided that they should postpone their probe into Rachel Carver's professional life until the following morning. They set off to Evesham hoping to be at the library for opening time, but, being a little delayed by an accident, it was nearer half past ten than ten o'clock when they entered the august precincts. They parked in the multi-storey car-park in Brick-kiln Street, cut through to the High Street and so into Oat Street. They had not announced their visit but hoped that the chief librarian would be able to spare them a little of her time. The young girl at the counter asked them to wait a few moments, disappeared into an office and reappeared followed by a mature woman of somewhat forbidding appearance, brisk and seemingly less than pleased to see them. When the inspector had impressed on her, in a few words, that their talk concerned the late Mrs Carver and should be private, she led them less than graciously back to the office whence she had emerged and invited them to be seated. She explained that, as they had still not been able to fill the vacancy created by Rachel's death, they were short-handed and pressed for time. She hoped they would excuse her peremptory manner. Her name was apparently Fortescue.

'Mrs Fortescue,' Wickfield began blandly enough. 'We shall take up as little of your time as possible. We have really only one question for you. You see, we have been investigating Mrs Carver's family background and personal relationships, and I confess to you that we are not finding it easy to identify anyone who might wish her such harm as to kill her. So we must now see whether there was anything in her professional life which could provide us with a lead. Would you be kind enough to tell us what you can about Rachel's time here? For example, how long had she worked at the library?'

'Quite a few years, Inspector. I've been here four years, and she was already here when I arrived.'

'Was she good at her work? Did she get on with the users of the library?'

'Oh, yes, I have no complaints. She was not exactly jolly, if you take my meaning, perhaps a little severe for my taste' – and that was saying quite a lot – 'but she was efficient and helpful with the customers.'

'Can you remember any incident that might have made her enemies?'

'Oh, no, Inspector, nothing like that, not in my time, at any rate. This is a quiet town, and I have never witnessed violence in the library in all my years here.'

'I wasn't exactly thinking of violence in the library, Mrs Fortescue. Had she offended a customer, put somebody's back up, perhaps?'

'No, no, that wouldn't be like Rachel at all,' the librarian answered with some vigour. 'I can, however, mention a certain matter to you which may or may not be relevant. Please take what I am about to tell you with great caution, because I may well be speaking out of turn. Rachel was not, well, she was not pretty, or even really very attractive – I speak as a woman, of course, Inspector, and my judgement is probably worth very little. She could also be rather morose, or preoccupied, as if she had other things on her mind than serving customers or helping about the place. On the other hand, she had a certain - what shall I say? – allure, a certain sexual appeal, particularly where older men were concerned. This was apparent to me, although I never picked up on it personally. Now recently – say, over the last six months – a customer seems to have become almost obsessed with her. He seems harmless enough, but his attachment to Rachel was somehow not very healthy, if you get my meaning. I mean, he must be well into his fifties, and she was only late twenties. Furthermore, she was a married woman and always wore a ring, so there could be no mistake about it.'

'Did she flirt with this man?' Wickfield asked. 'Did she lead him on?'

'No, no, Inspector, she seemed almost to ignore him, beyond, of course, helping him with his books. No, she seemed to be perfectly happily married. Playing the coquette would have been quite foreign to her.'

'Do you know how it all started?' Spooner asked.

'Yes, I do, as it happens. This particular customer, whom I knew by sight, came in one day, as I say about six months ago, and asked whether we had a particular book. Can't remember what it was: something by William Locke, I think. I remember the customer saying that you could rely on Locke – or perhaps it was Mason - to write a serious and interesting novel without a lot of sex and violence. Mind you,' Mrs Fortescue added in an undertone, 'Locke was writing between the wars, so he didn't have much choice. Anyway, it was Rachel who dealt with him, and he must have liked the treatment, because the following day he returned and spent time in the library browsing, taking several opportunities to speak to Rachel whenever she had a gap in the queue. Thereafter, long after his book had been delivered, he came in nearly every day and never left without speaking with Rachel.'

'And how did she take it?'

'She paid him no particular attention, I think I can truthfully say. She never led him on, certainly not in my hearing, and she was no more than correct with him - the same as with all our customers, I'll say that for her.'

Then Spooner asked Mrs Fortescue whether she got the

impression that this male customer was importuning the late Mrs Carver. 'Importuning? No, I shouldn't say so,' she replied. 'On the other hand, it takes a certain persistence to come in every day in order to have a few words with her. Is that importunate? No, just tenacious, perhaps. He was never unpleasant or overbearing with her in my presence.'

'So who is this gentleman, Mrs Fortescue? We shall have to see him as part of our inquiry.'

'His name is – hold on, Inspector – a rather unusual one. His surname is Peabody, and his Christian name, now let me see – yes, Grimwold, I think. Mr Grimwold Peabody, that's it.'

'Do you know where he lives?'

Mrs Fortescue walked over to a filing cabinet and leafed through the cards of library users.

'Here we are,' she announced. 'Mr G Peabody, 3 Montfort Street, Evesham. Do you want the telephone number, Inspector?'

'No, that won't be necessary, but we should appreciate general directions to Montfort Street.'

It made eminent sense to pay Mr Peabody a visit there and then. They urgently needed to make progress in the case, with the DCI champing at the bit, and with petrol not so cheap that the team could afford to run up and down to Evesham carelessly every day of the week. The odd numbers in Montfort Street were sufficiently shielded by the even houses not to be too troubled by the noise of the traffic on Elm Road. It was, in fact, part of a pleasant suburb, with neatly kept houses, trees in the streets, and a somnolent air. Mr Peabody proved to be a stiffly upright gentleman, looking sixty but, as they discovered, a few years younger, undoubtedly ex-forces, still clearly active and alert, but equally clearly retired: that he was at home during the day already suggested this. He was taken aback by the appearance of two policemen on his doorstep; he was thankful at least that they were not in uniform.

'What on earth is all this about, Gentlemen? I'm not aware of contravening the law of the land in any way whatever. I pay my taxes, I mind my own business, I do not intrude into my neighbours' lives. So how can I help you?'

'Mr Peabody, I believe all you say,' Wickfield replied, 'and I hasten to add that we're not calling because you're under suspicion of any crime. We just need to clarify a little matter which might be connected with a case on which we are working at the moment.'

'Oh, yes? Might that be Mrs Carver's death of last week? I heard they'd got the CID in.'

'You are right, Mr Peabody.'

'Where do I come into it, if I may ask?'

'You knew her, we understand.'

'Yes, I knew her. A lovely person. She was always so helpful to me when I went into the library.'

'We are told that there was a little more to it than that.'

'"A little more to it than that"? What is that supposed to mean, Inspector?'

'We understand you used to go into the library every day and make sure you had at least some conversation with Mrs Carver.'

'I suppose that old bat of a librarian told you.'

'Never mind who told us, Sir. Is it true?'

'And what if it is? Since when has it been a crime to talk to a library assistant?'

'It's not a crime, Sir, but we are investigating every aspect of Mrs Carver's life, and you might be able to help us. For example, did she ever mention to you being frightened of someone?'

Wickfield's change of tack took Peabody off his guard: from vague suspect he had suddenly become no more than a member of the public helping the police in their inquiries.

'No, Inspector. We never talked about personal things. It was always books, or general subjects like politics, occasionally religion, or the arts. She was both a good talker and a good listener. The trouble was that she never really had time to stop and talk properly. I don't blame her in the least, because, after all, she had her job to do, and she was conscientious, I can assure you.'

'Did you ever get the impression that she had something particular, perhaps something dangerous, on her mind?'

'Well, it's funny you should ask that, Inspector, because she always gave the impression, in the nicest possible way, of thinking of something else when she was talking to you.'

'Have you any idea what?'

'None whatever, I'm afraid. As I said, we never confided in each other: it wasn't that sort of relationship.'

'Would you have liked the relationship to develop, Mr Peabody?'

'Let me be quite frank with you, Inspector. I was very fond of Rachel, very fond indeed. She was always kind to me. I appreciated that. That she was rather distant didn't worry me at all: it was quite enough for me to be near her, but as for developing the relationship, as you put it, that was never on the cards. She was married, as of course you know. I couldn't do anything that would touch a marriage.'

Spooner then dipped into the conversation. 'Were you never married yourself, Mr Peabody?'

There was an embarrassed silence. Spooner did not quite understand how such an, as he thought, innocuous question could reduce a man, hitherto so voluble, to speechlessness. Peabody took his time.

'I don't quite see what that's got to do with our present business, Sergeant,' he offered finally, 'but I've no real objection to your knowing. You could always find out for yourselves if you wished, and I shouldn't want you to think I had deliberately concealed anything in my expressions of regard for Mrs Carver. You have probably guessed that I was in the army: I can't get the army out of my blood. I look army, don't I? In 1956 I was sent out to Kenya to help subdue the Mau Mau, when the emergency was already four years old. I knew nothing about the war other than what my superiors had told me. The Kikuyu were troublemakers, Kenyatta was stirring them up, the poor would be the first to suffer, the Kenyans would quickly revert to tribalism, cannibalism and savagery unless the Mau Mau were defeated, and so on. I dived into the fighting with relish. What were a few, or even many, black deaths compared with the glory of bringing civilisation to a backward people? We British set up what were called "free fire zones", where anybody could be shot with impunity – providing, of course, that he was black. Anyhow, I'd rather not go back over those terrible years: the hangings, the atrocities, the concentration camps, the brutalities of slave-labour – that's what it amounted to – the oppression of the local population, the injustices. The murder of eleven prisoners at Hola in 1959 thankfully induced the British authorities to change their policies, but by then I was far gone in bloodshed. Knowing nothing about the massacre at Hola, I committed an atrocity of my own. I was forty-six. The authorities decided to make an example of me, and I was cashiered. No ceremony, a summary dismissal from the army. I deserved it. I can offer no justification for what I did, and I have no resentment at my treatment on the army's part.

'When I got back to the United Kingdom, news of my disgrace had preceded me, and my wife of twenty years was gone. My two children refused to have anything to do with me, and I don't blame them. I have lived on my own ever since: a pariah, a burden to myself. And then Rachel came along: kind and detached and unquestioning. No thought of marriage entered my head, even had it been possible, because I couldn't saddle another kindly woman with the monster I had become.'

Wickfield let a few minutes of silence pass.

'Do you own a gun, Mr Peabody?' he then asked.

'No, wouldn't go near the things now.'

'So you don't know anything about the Hi-Power used to shoot Rachel?'

'Nothing. You don't seem to realise, Inspector, that that woman was a lifeline to me. Why on earth should I wish to harm her?'

'Just for the sake of completion, Sir, would you mind telling us where you were on the evening of Tuesday last, between four and six?'

'So I am a suspect after all, Inspector?'

'Not exactly, Mr Peabody, but we do need to satisfy the Chief Inspector that our investigation has been thorough.'

'Very well, I see that. Tuesday last? I was probably here at home.'

'Is there anyone that can confirm that, do you think?'

'I doubt it. Wait a minute, though. I did make a phone-call to my sister some time about then.'

'Any idea more precisely, Sir?'

'Well, my phone-company can tell you, or my sister probably, but I should think about five o'clock. I seem to remember listening to the five o'clock news and then phoning Julia.'

'Thank you, Mr Peabody, I don't think we need trouble you any more.'

When they had left Evesham, however, Wickfield asked his assistant to check on whether Peabody had a criminal record.

'There's something about that man that unsettles me,' he said. 'Can't put my finger on it. Did you get the same feeling, Sergeant?'

'No, Sir, can't say as I did. Seemed all above board to me. Mind you, he cuts a bit of a sad figure, doesn't he? Not yet sixty, yet all alone and probably bored out of his mind. It is sad to see him obliged by loneliness to drift into the library every day just to exchange a few casual words with a young woman thirty years his junior. And his war record can't be much of a comfort. We reap what we sow, I suppose. It's not God who repays, it's our own actions.'

'You been mugging up on your Hinduism, Sergeant?'

The report on Peabody was positive. Since his dismissal from the army twelve years before, he had several minor convictions for threatening behaviour and indecent exposure and cautions for verbal abuse. The man had been selective in his choice of misdeeds to lay before the police, presumably on the assumption that, if he were frank about one misdemeanour, they would not bother to look for others. The question Wickfield now asked himself was whether, despite his denials, Mr Grimwold Peabody had perhaps made an improper suggestion to Mrs Carver, had been rebuffed, and his *amour propre* had not allowed him to ignore it. Yet it did not seem a sufficient basis for murder.

Ten

*F*ive days had now passed since the discovery of Rachel Carver's body, six since her murder, and yet, despite vigorous, purposeful and intelligent activity on the part of Wickfield and Spooner, the team seemed no closer to a solution. Realising that the source of this seeming ineptitude was a failure to digest the information that they had so painstakingly gathered, Wickfield decided to convene a meeting at the highest level in order to seek a path through the maze. Accordingly, on the following morning, having already instructed his sergeant to prepare a balance sheet, Wickfield summoned Spooner to the Paradise Café in The Bow, and the two men settled down to a calm and systematic overview of the data. They were in striking contrast. The senior was big and bony, with a beak of a nose under shaggy eye-brows and a less than full mop of hair, disorderly dress, a vague, cogitative expression on his choppy features, whereas the junior was of a disciplined aspect, dapper, focused, of average build. The one complemented the other, and they knew it. So many cases had now come their way and been successfully pursued that they could be in no doubt that Wickfield's dogged perseverance and flashes of insight and Spooner's orderly, methodical but less intuitive approach to the matter in hand produced results of which their superiors could be proud, if not always sufficiently grateful. These two men, then, sat in a quiet corner of the establishment, on adjacent sides of a square table facing into the room. Since only a few early shoppers were as yet patronising the café at this hour, they had their corner to themselves, as desired.

'Right, Sergeant,' Wickfield began. 'Sock it to me. What have we got?'

'Well, Sir, this is going to take some time, as we seem to have interviewed half the population of Worcestershire, even though the only piece of concrete evidence we have is a gun. So please be patient, and feel free to order another pot of tea when we have exhausted this one. Thinking is thirsty work.'

Wickfield nodded.

'First of all, then, the facts. These seem to be few and easily summarised. Rachel Carver sets off one afternoon to plant on her victim the evidence of a building society robbery, namely, a fake gun and a bundle of cash. She gains access to her victim's house by using a key she had had made precisely for this occasion, plants the evidence, and leaves. At some point she meets her killer, is shot twice in the chest and dumped behind the Baptist chapel. Her handbag has not been found, but the weapon used to kill her is the Browning Hi-Power found in Michael Napier's wardrobe in place of the dummy supposedly put there by Rachel. That's about it. I should add, Sir, although I know you have spotted it but are too polite to say anything, these alleged facts are based partly on the husband's testimony, partly on surmise, and only partly on reality. My point is that we are not yet in a position to improve on this version of events. Do you agree, Sir?'

'Spooner, I am speechless with admiration. Please go on.'

Spooner paused to imbibe several long draughts of tea and to chew over a piece of scone.

'Before I come on to any sort of speculation, let me just run through the testimony of those we have interviewed, bearing in mind that some, or possibly all, of them are lying energetically through their back teeth. First of all, we interviewed Michael Napier, after an anonymous female tip-off which we later discovered was, in all probability, the less-than-subtle work of Rachel Carver. We saw him twice. On the first occasion, on the Wednesday of the discovery of the body, he told us about the previous occasion on which he had been framed for a robbery on a jeweller's shop, for which he went down for two months. In connexion with the present events, he was not at home, but in a pub drinking with a friend, when the building society evidence was planted on him, the perpetrator presumably using a false key to gain entry. He confesses to being completely mystified, as well he might. At the second interview, conducted by yourself, Sir, on the following day, Napier exculpated himself from any involvement in Rachel's murder by providing solid alibis. He admitted that he had been interviewed by the police in 1951 when Len Appleton was murdered, but only because of a tenuous connexion with the dead man dating back to primary-school days and because of being called Michael – hardly his fault. So far, so good. We thus appear to have a man of Rachel Carver's remote circle of acquaintances caught up in a plot to discredit him, for no reason he can fathom.

'Then we approached the grieving husband, Andrew Carver, Andy to his friends, a local baker's assistant. Again, he was interviewed on two occasions, once on the Wednesday, once on the Thursday. It was only at the second interview, which I undertook, that he revealed Rachel's supposed identification of her father's killer through recognising his voice and the plans to punish Napier by framing him for crimes of which he was innocent. Carver also, under some very subtle questioning – all right, he was asked outright - produced alibis for the time of Rachel's murder.

'That first day, the Wednesday, we also interviewed Mrs Bernard Platt, née Appleton, Rachel's aunt Sarah who had brought her up with her own children from when she was five. It was through her that we first learnt that her brother Leonard had been murdered. She also cautioned against taking seriously Rachel's alleged memory of the familiar name Mick. And if I may interject here, Sir, I'm not sure we've taken sufficient account of her warning. However, I'll return to that in due course.

'Then you, Sir, jetted off to Spain to question Napier's brother Victor.'

'You make it sound like a holiday, Sergeant. I was working, let me tell you, and I didn't enjoy the experience, because Victor and I didn't really hit it off. On the other hand, Mrs Victor was – how shall I put it? – a rather engaging woman; yes, a very personable and attractive specimen of the human female. However, go on.'

'Well, according to your notes, Sir, Victor admitted knowing Len Appleton in later life, that is, after their school-days, being interviewed by the police concerning his murder, moving to Spain at about the same time, divorcing his wife of the time and remarrying a couple of years back. No reason why he shouldn't, of course. He also admitted being in England on a visit to his oldest brother Noel at the time of Rachel's murder. He also had things to say, not all of them positive, about his other brother Michael, notably his shabby treatment of his wife Trudy. He is able to provide a partial alibi for the time of Rachel Carver's murder.

'While you were cavorting round the Mediterranean – sorry, Sir, while you were painfully engaged in police work in the south of Spain – I found out some information on the Appleton family. Neither Leonard's nor Rachel's money affairs seem to offer any purchase for an accusation of murder.

'We were then, after the weekend, bounced into an interview with the eccentric Giles Sercombe, whose main purpose was to tell us about suspicions that Michael Napier murdered his wife, by strangulation, and concealed the body, giving out to his acquaintances that she had left him, he knew not why or whither. The reverend could offer no evidence, just hearsay, but felt it to be his duty to call us.

'Two more interviews followed that same Monday, one conducted by you, Sir, and one by me. You went to see the eldest of the three Napier brothers, Noel, who is not seriously under suspicion, partly because his name doesn't have an -ic sound. He gave us three pieces of information. One, Victor's alibi for the previous Tuesday afternoon could be substantiated from 5.15 onwards. Two, Noel and his wife were uncertain about Trudy's fate, as Victor had been previously. Three, Trudy was liked by some of the family, very much disliked by others. None of this amounted to very much – with respect, Sir, I'm sure.'

'Yes, yes, Spooner, cut out the flattery. Get on with the story. Your exposition is, as always, admirably clear otherwise.'

'While you were drinking tea in the comfortable country home of Mr and Mrs Noel Napier – sorry, Sir, I shall rephrase that: while you were slogging away at the public edge of detective duties – '

'Sergeant, just get on with it, will you?'

'Yes, Sir, of course, Sir - I interviewed Mrs Harriet Cosgrove, formerly Mrs Victor Napier, in Droitwich. Although at one time married to our Spanish Victor, she had also known, naturally, his two older brothers, although not intimately at the time of Leonard

Appleton's death. She came up with one or two small pieces of information that might be useful. For example, she couldn't visualise any of the brothers in the role of murderer, and she did confirm that neither Noel nor Victor seemed to have kept up much with Leonard after school. On the other hand, she admitted that Victor had gone to Leonard for a loan and been refused. She also shed a different light on our friend Michael, whom she liked. Trudy she dismissed as a "fishwife". Dearie me, the way these people talk.'

'That's nothing to the purpose, Sergeant. Please proceed.'

'Yes, Sir. We then felt we had exhausted, for the time being, the possibilities of the Appleton and Napier families, and we pursued an inquiry into Rachel Carver's working life. This led us to the not altogether savoury Grimwold Peabody, cashiered army major, who might be suspected of a crush on poor Rachel. Peabody has a rather flimsy alibi for the time of Rachel's murder, but he claims not to own a 9 mm Browning.'

Spooner paused for further copious draughts of rapidly cooling tea and several more morsels of scone. Another pot was ordered and delivered to the table. A few more shoppers came and went, but Wickfield and Spooner, pleasantly engaged in the serious business of detection, sat on. Spooner turned a few leaves of his spiral-bound notepad, cleared his throat and continued his exposition.

'We don't yet know exactly what happened, beyond, of course, the fact of poor Mrs Carver's murder. We're not very clear on motive, but at least we have a small number of suspects, all male, and eventually one of these may be persuaded to spill the beans.'

'"Spill the beans", Sergeant?' Wickfield said as he laughed. However, seeing the look of surprise that Spooner gave, he straightened his face and said, 'Please continue, Sergeant. I apologise for the interruption.'

'If we accept Rachel's remembrance of "Mick" or similar, we have the Napier brothers Michael and Victor. If, on the other hand, we dismiss that as a serious mishearing of some completely different expression, we are left with the outsider Grimwold Peabody. By the way, Sir, where on earth do you think his parents dredged that name up from? Must be an invention, surely? Or perhaps his real name is Ronald or Denis, and he wanted to soup it up a bit.

'Anyway, let's start with Michael. What would his motive be? If we go along with Andrew Carver, Rachel recognised him as the man who murdered her father and decided to set him up for a couple of lesser crimes by way of punishment. Perhaps she intended further outrages in the future: we may never know. Let us say Michael cottoned on to the persecution. It would then be in his interest to delete Rachel. Added to this is suspicion sown by his neighbour and channelled to us by the good offices of the Reverend Giles Sercombe that he murdered his wife Trudy, who disappeared eight or nine years ago. By the way, Sir, that might be worth following up if Michael is the front-runner in our quest for Rachel's murderer. Against this are the facts that he proclaims his innocence, he has never been known as Mick, and he has an unassailable alibi.

'On to Victor. That you took against Victor when you visited him in Spain is a strong indication of his guilt. Sorry, Sir, no flattery: I forgot. I'll try again. Victor is in the frame because he left Worcester at about the time of Appleton's murder in 1951, he was in Evesham when Rachel Carver was shot and his alibi is shaky, and his first wife tells us he had business dealings with Appleton which came to nothing and which might have been the basis for resentment.'

'Just let me interrupt a moment, Sergeant. His present wife is elegant and charming. Surely she wouldn't have married a monster? Doesn't her choice of husband speak in his favour?'

'Yes, of course, Sir, but we mustn't let our prejudices get in the way of our wiser judgement - must we, Sir?'

'No, no, of course not,' Wickfield said, as a beguiling image of the svelte Kimberly crossed his line of vision, 'I stand corrected. Please continue. I promise I shan't interrupt again.' Spooner acknowledged this confession of repentance, took a few seconds to pick up the threads of his discourse and continued.

'These two suspects fit in with the young Rachel's remembrance, but how solid is that remembrance? The girl was five years old, she was frightened, probably confused by what was happening, and she admits that the gist of the conversation passed her by. Well, at five years old, it would, wouldn't it? Furthermore, her aunt, probably the person in the world who knew her best, is happy to put a completely different construction on the sound "-ick". In short, I don't think we should set much store by Rachel here. And another thing: can we seriously believe that the girl remembered a voice from the age of five to the age of twenty-seven? It strains our credulity rather, doesn't it, Sir?

'So finally we come to Peabody, who cuts a sad figure, in my opinion, although of course I mustn't let that feeling cloud my judgement – Sir.'

Wickfield acknowledged this sally with a slight nod.

'It's all hypothesis here. We know he was attracted to Rachel, almost besotted, one might say. He claims that his feelings and actions were completely gentlemanly, but we could easily surmise that his feelings tipped over into obsession, that he was rebuffed, and that he took his revenge. His alibi is – well, essentially he hasn't got one, because even if he did make a phone-call at five o'clock, the rest of the window – 4.15 to 5.45 - is unaccounted for. We know also, on his own admission and from his police record, that he has been guilty of violence in the past. We have no independent verification that he did not own a pistol, and one might almost say that the balance of probabilities, given his background, is that he did. Perhaps that is an unfair comment, however. In Peabody's favour is the discovery of the gun in Napier's wardrobe. How could he have had anything to do with that?

'A fourth suspect is the husband, although, from the information we have gathered, the odds against him are long. And that's about it, Sir.'

Wickfield and Spooner sat in silence for a while, the latter doodling on his note-book, the former pensive.

'Thank you for that, Sergeant. To which of the suspects do you incline, may I ask?'

'Well, you must remember that I haven't met Victor, so I'm not really in a position to comment on him, but I'd probably go for Peabody.'

'Mm,' Wickfield commented with an understated lack of commitment.

When nothing further was forthcoming, Spooner invited him to give a further opinion.

'Oh, I really don't know, Sergeant. It's between Michael and Peabody, but how are we to solve the puzzle on which you have put your trusty finger, namely, the presence of the gun in Napier's house?'

'Well, let's do a bit of creative reconstruction, shall we, Sir, to answer my own question? Peabody meets Rachel in town, by design or by accident. He has come for a final show-down: either she leaves her husband for Peabody or he shoots himself.'

'This is a bit dramatic, isn't it, Sergeant?'

'Yes, Sir – I mean, no, Sir. Stranger things than this have happened. Any way, as they talk, she reveals that she is on her way to Michael Napier's house to plant the evidence that will convict him, and she appeals for Peabody's help. They are on their way to Bridge Street via Oat Street and Cowl Street – because it's quieter that way. Afraid of being recognised round Montfort Street, she gives Peabody the evidence and the spare key to Napier's house, asks him to do the necessary and prepares to leave. He appeals to her. "Come away with me, darling. I love you madly, passionately. You are the only sparkle in my life. I cannot live without you." "No, sorry, Mr Peabody, I'm happily married, and in any case I'm not in love with you." "What does your love matter? I have enough for the two of us." "Go away, Grimwold, I'm not interested." "Please, please, I shall shoot myself if you refuse." "For the last time, you horrible man, leave me alone. I never wish to see you again." "Right, if I can't have you, nobody else will. Come with me," and he drags her into the cul-de-sac, Seward Close, in which the Baptist chapel is situated. She gets frightened and begins to resist. So he shoots her. He drags the body round the back of the church – it would already be dark at this time, with only the flare of street-lamps to illuminate the ghastly deed - hares it up to Poplar Close, plants the gun and cash and saunters back home.'

'Steady on, Sergeant, this is a real murder we're talking about, not some television thriller. But it won't do.'

'Why won't it do, Sir?'

'Because if he shot her in Cowl Street, somebody would have heard.'

'Not necessarily, Sir. If they were standing at the entrance to Seward Close, they would have been shielded from the houses behind by the chapel, and from the street by the archway. How much sound does a Hi-Power make? No more than a lawn-mower coughing – '

'What: in December?'

' – or a car back-firing.'

'Ye-e-s,' Wickfield said doubtfully. 'It's just possible, I suppose.'

'Let's say Peabody and Rachel met in the High Street five minutes after Rachel left home,' said Spooner, warming to his theme. 'That's 4.20. They stroll, they talk, she tells him about her designs on Napier. That's 4.35, and by this time they are in Cowl Street. By 4.40 it's all over. Peabody crosses the river, calls at Napier's house to plant the evidence – not of Napier's crime only, but of his own – and walks back to his own house, which is only five minutes from Napier's. He is still in plenty of time to phone his sister at 5.0. Did you notice, Sir, how we had to drag the alibi out of him: a very convincing show of innocence?'

'And what happened to Rachel's handbag and the fake gun?'

'Peabody put them under his coat and later that night dropped them in the river – where they will be found in the mud to this very day.'

'How do you propose to prove this colourful hypothesis?'

'Ah, there you have me. We could appeal for witnesses up and down Cowl Street. Any of the residents, or a passer-by, may have seen or heard something.'

'Yes, I think we have neglected to do that.'

'Otherwise, I'm not sure we're ever going to be able to. Perhaps this is one of those cases where we have to leave the punishment to God.'

'For crying out loud, Spooner, we're policemen, not theologians. We've got to do our best to nail the killer, but if we accept Peabody as the murderer of Rachel Carver, for motives of lust and broken pride, where do we go with the murder of Leonard Appleton?'

'Well, Sir, we're not any forrader with that, but it's not really our job to investigate it, is it? After all, our colleagues did what they could twenty years ago and drew a blank. We're not really in a position to improve on their record, I should have thought.'

'No, maybe you're right at that. On the other hand, your exposition, admirable in its succinctness and clarity as always – ahem, ahem - has suggested several lines we haven't yet pursued, whether or not the two murders are connected.'

'Let me guess, Sir. We need to chase up what happened to Trudy Napier, and we need to check for witnesses in Cowl Street. The gun might also be an important lead. Anything else?'

'Well, there is one avenue that hasn't even occurred to us so far. Leonard Appleton had a sister Claire who married, in your words, a "wastrel" called Edwin Jones. Do you think that might yield something? Claire and Edwin are as close to Appleton as aunt Sarah, and I think we have neglected them. Perhaps the wastrel Edwin is the candidate that Providence has lined up for us.'

Eleven

Miss – or perhaps more properly Ms – Shilling lived alone in an isolated cottage on the edge of the reservoir. The reservoir had been created in the last years of the nineteenth century to provide a water-source for the growing demands of the city of Perth – the Scottish city, quondam capital of the country, not its Australian namesake. (Although still quite attractive in its way, with parks fore and aft and a pleasurable use of the river, Perth is a shadow of its former self: stripped of its city walls, the castle, the Earl of Gowrie's mansion and other prestigious constructions, it has been spoilt, not despite, but because of, the planners' best intentions. None of this is relevant in the present context!) A natural dip in the Ochil Hills was dammed and flooded to create a sizeable lake. No houses or important agricultural land had been destroyed, and just one croft remained, untouched above the water-line, to remind walkers – the few walkers – that this land had long supported a permanent crofter. The narrow road from the village that permitted access to the water-works at the lower end of the reservoir also enabled Miss Shilling to reach her modest dwelling. From the water-works she was obliged to dismount from her bicycle and wheel it over a rough path that led round the lake to her cottage on the eastern side. She had rescued a small plot of land from the surrounding heather to provide a vegetable garden, with a stone wall (ably repaired) and netting to keep the voracious rabbits at bay, but despite green manuring, the soil was poor and her crops thin. She descended once a week to the village to stock up with supplies, filling her panniers with groceries and flour. In the summer and autumn, covering considerable distances, she gathered blueberries and blackberries, wild

103

strawberries and raspberries, mushrooms and crab-apples, hazelnuts, rosehips, and a variety of leaves in lieu of more conventional vegetables. She kept three chickens. She trapped rabbits, using a wire noose attached to a peg and set across a run; she trapped pheasants using a simple gadget made of a length of six-inch piping and some chicken-wire. Miss Shilling was resourceful. Miss Shilling was regarded locally with some awe, as being a strange creature closer to nature than to her fellow-humans. No one ever ventured on to the hillsides to pay her a visit. This was a pity, because, although she was undoubtedly acid and saturnine, there was much good and much wisdom in her.

From the front of her cottage, she could look out over the water below her to the woods on the other side of the reservoir and beyond them to the gentle, rounded hill-tops that ran on, out of sight, to Stirling. Above all, the almost unbroken silence attracted and soothed her. She understood that modern farming required the use of machinery, but the intrusive noise irked her none the less. The westward view was one in which she frequently revelled: not world-class, but gentle and reassuring, millennial and changeless, a classic landscape of the Scottish uplands.

She was reclining one day in a deck-chair in front of her cottage, facing into the late summer sun and enjoying the immense silence of the hills, when a walker, leaning on a stick, came into view on the footpath. Looking ashen grey, he hobbled over to her garden and asked whether she could spare a cup of tea.

'I suddenly don't feel so good,' he murmured apologetically.

'Sit down,' she answered summarily. 'I shan't be a jiffy. What about a glass of water first?'

'That would be very welcome,' he managed to say.

As he rested and sipped his water, colour began to tinge his cheeks.

'I'm so sorry to put you to this trouble,' he said eventually. 'I set off for a short walk by the reservoir, and somehow I must have overdone it.'

'Don't you worry,' she said. 'You'll be better in a minute, and then I can go with you back down the hill. You've come up from Damhead, I take it?'

'Yes, yes. Perhaps it's the heat.'

There were a few minutes of silence as Miss Shilling disappeared into her kitchen to fetch a mug of tea and a biscuit.

'Do you usually walk this far?' she asked, producing a kitchen chair for herself to sit on.

'Oh, Lord, yes. I usually stick to the metalled road, either into Candy Glen or up and then down to Path of Condie, but today the weather was so fine I thought I would get off the roads for a bit. One of my favourite spots as a youth was Deas' Cairn. You'll know it, of course?'

'Oh, yes,' she said appreciatively. 'Magnificent views on a clear day. And that was where I first encountered that Scots word "stank", meaning a pool or pond. It was on my walking map. I've always thought what a strange word it seems to the English person. You're obviously local, then.'

'Born here, retired here, but I moved away for years. I was delighted to be able to return. That's a few years ago now, and of course I couldn't buy back the house was I born in – even if I'd wanted to, but I'm very happy back at my roots. And what about yourself? You're not local, are you?'

'No, I'm not. Well, not really.'

'What do you mean?' he asked as he sipped his tea, cradling the mug with both hands.

'Well,' she explained, 'my parents bought this cottage fifty years ago, did it up and used it as a holiday home. I used often to come here as a child. They died, and I was left with a large house and this cottage. So I decided a year or two ago to rent out the big house, live on the rental and retire to this place.'

'You must get lonely,' he said.

'Not often,' she answered. 'I never really got on with people. I'm too short-tempered, too suspicious of people's motives, too easily bored by trite conversations.'

When he looked slightly pained, she hastened to add that she did not find him boring.

'No, once in a while it makes a pleasant change to talk to a human rather than to the crows. Most of the time, I never see anyone. If I go down to the village, I may chat a bit with the folks in the shop, or the joiner across from the shop, but it's really only to pass the time of day.'

'Do you never attend the church in the village? That would introduce you to people. No, sorry, I shouldn't be asking that: much too personal a question!'

She laughed a little.

'I can see *you* don't,' she said, 'otherwise you'd know the answer to that question!'

He smiled ruefully. 'No, I don't go. I know I must look like an old stodge to you, but even I find services dated. However, I do listen to religious programmes on the wireless. It's not that I'm not interested. You know, what really disheartens me is the obstinacy with which churches and ministers stick with the King James version of the Bible. I have always understood that the New Testament in particular was written by ordinary people, in their ordinary language: common Greek, not classical Greek; not by scholars for a refined readership in the polished language of the educated. Why, oh why do we petrify the text at 1611 instead of using a version accessible to the ordinary worshipper? As for modern worship, it is virtually unchanged since the Reformation. Have sensibilities and expectations not progressed beyond that? To enjoy modern worship you'd have to think they hadn't. Sorry, I'm probably being offensive. Please forgive me.'

'Not at all. Let's have another pot of tea,' she said, as she saw his empty mug waving about somewhat uncertainly.

'Don't mind if I do,' he said, offering his empty mug with, on its side, the legend 'Look Busy – Jesus is Coming'. Conversation lapsed as she disappeared to rustle up another brew from the interior of the cottage. The elderly gentleman sat on, quietly enjoying the warm sun and the views over the reservoir and the wooded hills beyond. There was, he well knew, a slightly more frequented footpath on the other side of the loch – reservoir, he supposed he should call it - but the views from it were more restricted because of the woods through which it passed for much of its length. He loved the gentle hills of his youth, although he acknowledged that the area could not rightly be thought particularly attractive to tourists.

'What do you do with yourself all day, if I may ask?' he said when she returned with fresh mugs.

'Well,' she replied, 'living mostly without packets and tins means I have to spend a lot of time preparing food from scratch. I walk. I have books and a piano. I listen to the wireless. Above all, I suppose, I think! What about you?'

'Oh, I potter. I listen to music a lot, I take walks, I do a spot of gardening, I read – although my eyes aren't what they were. But tell me, you say you think: what do you think about?'

'Life, what it all means' – she swept her hand round in a generous arc encompassing, as it might be, the entire globe. 'Is it all a random nothingness, or is there some steely purpose behind it?'

'And what good will it do you to find the answers?' he asked with a genuine inquiry in his voice. 'I'm not sure there are any answers, you know.'

'Oh, there are,' she came in quickly. 'It all depends on whether you find those answers helpful. Some people stare at the answers and don't know what to do with them. Answers require action, you see, so it's a much softer option to go on questioning and then shoving the questions to the back of one's mind. That saves you *doing* anything, but to the person who cares about the answers, they are a constant source of teasing delight. Thinking-time is never wasted time, you know.'

'Perhaps not, but does it ever help you to be a better person? That's what counts, surely?'

'Look, Mr – er?'

'Jack.'

'Look, Jack, I'm not quite sure why I'm telling you this, but you seem to be an understanding sort of person. Years ago I did something foolish – hasty – hurtful – and I have been debating ever since whether I can reverse it, and if I can, whether I should. Because I think mainly so that I can decide on the best course of action, I'm not engaged in idle riddles or abstruse speculations: there is purpose in my thinking, although heaven knows, after eight years, you'd think I should be getting somewhere! Does that meet your requirement?'

Sensing that there were deep waters here, Jack asked gently whether she would like to tell him about it.

'There's not much to tell, really,' she said, 'and I'm sure it can be of no interest to you.'

'Look,' he said, 'we're sitting comfortably in the sun, admiring the gorgeous view and enjoying each other's company for a while. Why not get it off your chest? It can't do any harm, surely, and it might just help.'

'I was married,' she said, 'and eight years ago I left my husband. I've been wondering ever since whether I did the right thing. That's about the size of it.'

'May I ask why you left him?'

'Oh, I don't know. Lack of self-confidence, I suppose, mainly.'

'What do you mean?'

'Jack, I'm not a nice person. I know I was difficult to live with: prickly, nagging, hard to please. I came to the conclusion my husband would be better off without me; so I left.'

'And you've been punishing yourself all these years by living like a hermit? But, my dear, you can safely leave the punishing to God. "Revenge is mine" and all that. Your business now is to grasp his mercy and his lovingkindness, surely? Tell me, if you were an intolerable burden on your husband, what was he like to you?'

'In a way, I suppose he was as bad – not an easy man to live with at all, but I was not responsible for his half of the marriage, was I? I was responsible for my half, and I let him down.'

'Do you still love him?'

'Yes, I think I do.'

'You think you do. Can you explain?' He sensed she had more to say.

'I do love him, still and always, but I'm not sure that love is the prime consideration. I tend to think in terms of my duties. I vowed to be his wife, and I was just too selfish to be any good at it. I failed, and I'm now frightened that, if I offer to go back, he'll reject me, and I shall feel even worse than I do now. Over the years that I've been on my own, thinking, wondering, worrying, I have begun to realise that the longer I leave it, the less the chance there is of our ever getting together again. I know that now. Yet I lack the strength, the determination, - the guts, really - to do anything about it. So I carry on here, and I suppose I shall die here.'

A few tears gathered in the corner of her eyes.

'Oh, Jack,' she said vehemently, 'what do you think I should do? What would you do if you were in my shoes?'

'Ah, but, you see, I'm not in your shoes, and I should be very foolish to attempt to advise you. But let me ask you this: you're obviously not fully happy here; what would be involved in getting in touch with your husband? Do you know where he's living?'

'In the same old house, I imagine.'

'Does he know where you are? Could he get in touch with you?'

'He probably guesses I'm here, but why would he get in touch with me when I made it quite clear that I wanted no more to do with him?'

'So let us say you write to him. What would you wish to tell him?'

'I would apologise for letting him down. I would promise to try harder in future. I would ask whether he would have me back.'

'Could he have got himself another woman in the meantime?'

'Possibly – even probably – but we've never divorced, so he can't have married again.'

'What if he says yes to you?'

'I should return post haste.'

'And how easy would you find it to change if he's the same? You'd simply bicker again, wouldn't you?'

'I'd do my level best not to. I know I've changed over the last eight years.'

'And what if he said no?'

'I'd be condemned to stay here on my own for ever. I suppose I'd have to get used to it. Are you married, Jack?'

'I'm a widower. The loneliness is almost unbearable sometimes. Perhaps I should correct that: it's not company in general I lack – it's the company of one person in particular, and there's nothing anybody can do about that.'

A melancholy silence descended on the pair, each deeply wrapped in painful thoughts.

'Let me put you another question,' the old gentleman resumed. 'You're frightened your husband may say no, and that would be worse for you than not knowing. How could it be worse?'

'At the moment I can live in hope. A no would dash that hope.'

'But you've as good as admitted you're not happy as you are. You think, you wonder, you turn things over and over in your mind. Why would a refusal be harder to bear than that?'

She looked at him with a soft, appreciative understanding in her eyes, but instead of speaking, she simply shook her head in doubt.

'Maybe you're right,' she said at length. 'Maybe I should make an effort and see what happens. You've been so understanding, thank you.'

'It's sometimes good to talk, you know. You can't cut yourself off completely from others, especially when you're faced with a difficulty. But I'm serious when I say that I cannot advise you: the decision has to be yours, because you are the only one in possession of all the relevant facts, but I feel very much for you and only wish I could help more.'

'Were you happily married, Jack?'

'Yes, blissfully. We had our differences, of course – who doesn't? – but we fitted like hand and glove. Anyway, I've stacks and stacks of memories, and that's a huge consolation in my loss.'

The two of them, the middle-aged woman and the elderly gentleman, sitting side by side in an immensity of uninhabited countryside, strangers until a few hours ago, chatted companionably until the afternoon was far gone.

'Good heavens!' Jack said, as the sun began to dip below the facing hills, 'I must get on. My neighbour's expecting me for tea, and at this rate I shall be very late. Please excuse me.'

He refused his friend's offer to accompany him down into the glen, on the grounds that he was quite revived, thanks to her and her companionship. He wished her well in her continued deliberations and expressed the hope that, whatever decision she came to, she would find contentment in abiding by it. He promised to return on some future occasion.

'By the way,' he said as they parted, 'I still don't know your first name.'

'Believe it or not,' she said, as if an apology for an old-fashioned name made the news any the less unpalatable, 'it's Gertrude – but everyone calls me Trudy.'

Twelve

*W*ickfield was becoming increasingly despondent about his inability to identify Rachel Carver's murderer. He was not so concerned about her father's murderer, although, naturally, killing two birds with the same stone would be gratifying. His responsibility did not stretch back twenty years. The leads they were about to investigate were not very promising, and, if they were negative, he was not sure what courses of action would be left open to him. Surely he was not destined to tell the Chief Inspector, Sorry, we've got nowhere, please put me on another case, or Sorry, this is beyond me, please demote me to sergeant.

'Right, Sergeant, let's get going,' Wickfield announced with a flourish. 'You're going to find witnesses in Cowl Street, while I try to worm out of Michael Napier the truth of what happened to his missus. Then we are both going to visit Mr and Mrs Jones, aka Aunt Claire and her husband Edwin. You take a couple of uniform with you, although you'd probably do better to wait until the early evening, and I'll see you back here – when we can make it.'

Once more, Wickfield found himself driving down Worcester to Evesham. For a change he chose the A44, but at that time of day it proved just as exasperating as the B4084, and moreover a less attractive road from the point of view of pastoral scenery. Because it was Tuesday, he thought he would meet his quarry in the Golden Wheatsheaf, even though it meant dislodging his drinking-companion for a time. As he entered the public house, he saw Napier and his friend seated near the fire. He approached, excused himself, asked whether it would be convenient to have a few words with Mr

Napier, went to the bar to order a pint and returned to the waiting Napier. If the latter experienced any trepidation at the approaching encounter, certainly nothing of it was visible in his demeanour.

'Inspector,' he said, 'this is a great pleasure. To what do I owe the honour of yet further time in your company?'

Wickfield had rehearsed his opening comments, which could not reveal the source of his information but which, at the same time, could not be so bland that Napier could duck out of a firm answer to Wickfield's questioning.

'You are very kind to say so,' he began. 'Let me tell you that I am going back over Leonard Appleton's death again, because I still think a clue to Rachel's murder lies there somewhere. Now at that time, if I've got it right, you were already married.'

Recognising that this was more of a question than a statement, Napier nodded in agreement.

'Now I'm not sure that your wife – Trudy, wasn't it? – can add anything to what the police discovered from you and your brothers, but the fact is, she wasn't interviewed at the time, and it is just possible she may know something that, put together with other aspects of the case, may be helpful. So I'm anxious to trace her if I can, just for the sake of completion. We've already seen your sisters-in-law Shirley and Harriet. Can you think of any possible way in which we can trace Trudy?'

'Yes, Inspector, I can. If you and I go to my house now, I think we shall find her in, cooking supper.'

'What?' Wickfield's surprise got the better of him. He was stunned into the utterance of a single word. 'Your wife Trudy is at home at this minute cooking supper? Is that what you said?'

'Inspector, there's no need to be so surprised. We are married, you know, and have been for twenty years.'

'Yes, but I thought – '

'What you thought is nothing to the purpose now, Inspector. Come home and meet Trudy: she will be glad to make your acquaintance.' With that he finished his drink, urged the inspector to do likewise and made for the exit. They drove in separate cars and in a few minutes were at no.5 Poplar Close, where the curtains were drawn and the lights on inside and in the porch. The front-door was not locked. Napier ushered Wickfield into the hall.

'Trudy, darling, we have a visitor,' he shouted towards the kitchen. A smiling woman emerged from the house's nether regions, an apron round her waist. She was wiping her hands on a towel.

'Hello,' she said in a friendly tone. 'Have you come for supper? Because if you have, you are very welcome.'

Wickfield was so stunned that he stood there for a moment, giving very little evidence of his usual gentlemanly *sang-froid*. He managed to stammer that no, that was very kind, but he had not come to supper. On the other hand, could she spare him a few minutes on some other occasion, when it was more convenient for her than clearly it was now? At her quizzical look, Napier hastened to make proper introductions.

'No time like the present then, Inspector. The supper won't spoil for the sake of a few minutes, though perhaps you won't mind sitting in the kitchen. Mike, you go and change, and the inspector and I can talk while I keep an eye on things down here.'

Wickfield stepped into the kitchen and was greeted by the warm domestic scene of a table laid for two and supper cooking on the stove.

'Sit down, Inspector. You mustn't stand on ceremony here. Now what can I do for you?'

By this time the inspector had himself in hand, although his mind was racing with the implications of this unexpected encounter.

'Mrs Napier, may I just clarify one thing, and I hope you won't take this amiss. I had understood from your husband that – '

'Say no more, Inspector. Yes, I had gone away, but now I'm back. I came back at the weekend, after nine years in the wilderness. We have made up, and we are starting again.'

'But I saw your brother-in-law Noel yesterday, and he said nothing about it.'

'No, he wouldn't. Nobody knows yet – not until we get more used to each other's company.'

'I see. Well, Mrs Napier, you may be unaware that a certain Mrs Andrew Carver was found murdered in the town last week. You may remember her as little Rachel Appleton, daughter of Leonard who was killed in 1951. She was five at the time.'

'Yes, I remember.'

'Now you had just married Michael, and Michael was interviewed at the time, because he knew the Appletons, but you weren't – at least not according to the police record.'

'No, but then I had nothing to contribute, so nothing was lost.'

'Did you know the Appletons?'

'Yes, slightly. You see, he was a well-known businessman, and he married a local beauty. They were always featuring in the local papers and appearing at this or that function in the town. It would have been hard not to know them.'

'No, I mean, did you know them personally?'

'Well, I met them a couple of times, but that was all.'

'Through Michael?'

'No, not really. It was through Claire, his younger sister. I had some trouble with an elbow, went to the doctor and was sent to the hospital for some physio. It happened to be Claire who dealt with me.'

'Did you have any ideas about Leonard's death?'

'Oh, no, I didn't know the family well enough for that. I knew only what the papers said, and that wasn't much.'

Wickfield had perforce to leave the conversation there, unproductive though it was in most respects. He returned in a ruminative mood to the station, to find Spooner, hotfoot from Cowl Street, waiting to deliver his report.

'Well, Sergeant, any joy?'

'A minute scrap, Sir. We did the street systematically – '

'Of course: I should expect nothing less.'

' – going down both sides in the afternoon and back again in the evening to houses where we had found no one at home earlier on.'

'Good, good.'

'The thing is, no one remembers anything. There was no bang of which anyone would say, Oh, dear, a gun going off somewhere! or, That car sounds sick! And the cartridge-cases haven't been found either. If, as we have surmised, Rachel could have been shot in the street, you'd expect some sign of the cartridge to turn up. But no, nothing. This must mean either that Rachel was shot elsewhere, or that the killer made time to pick the cartridges up and made off with them. The fact that no unusual bang was heard, and the lack of cartridge-cases, suggest to me, Sir, that Rachel wasn't killed in Cowl Street.'

'Well, that's as may be,' Wickfield said, 'but you've still got to explain how her body got behind the chapel. When was it put there? Who put it there, and how did he manage it without being seen?'

'Well, Sir, I've thought about that – '

'Ah, I guessed you would have done.'

' - and I've come up with a little theory.'

'Excellent, Spooner. Let's be having it, then: don't leave me in suspense.'

'It's not actually very difficult to imagine the scene, Sir. As you know, the chapel is set back in a short dead-end street, facing out towards Cowl Street. In front there is parking for half-a-dozen cars, three on each side, with a turning space in between. The killer, with Rachel's body in the boot, drives confidently along Cowl Street, backs without hesitation into Seward Close, parks, carries the body behind the chapel and drives off again. Three things work in his favour, on which he may or may not have counted consciously. Firstly, it was a dark winter's evening, with distant figures and car number-plates difficult to read with any certainty. Secondly, there wouldn't be many people around at that time of evening – whatever time it was exactly – and in any case, even if anybody had been around, he'd have been very unlucky to attract attention just by backing into a cul-de-sac for a few moments. Thirdly, if he knew the area well, there would be no hesitation: he could have accomplished his grim task in minutes, if not seconds, moving in familiar surroundings. Doesn't all this mean that our friend Peabody is no longer in the picture? We have supposed that he didn't meet his victim in a car.'

'No, I don't think so. The fact that nobody remembers seeing or hearing anything unusual is merely negative: it doesn't mean that nothing unusual happened. Perhaps friend Peabody is guilty but was lucky enough not to be seen or heard in the act. You have, however, set in train yet another line of inquiry of which I hadn't thought. We really need to be examining the cars of our suspects searching for the slightest piece of evidence that Rachel's body was carried in the boot or possibly in the back. Shall we never come to the end of this inquiry?'

'I suppose that was a rhetorical question, Sir?'

'Yes, it was, Spooner. Thank you for your confidence. But we're going to get on to the next avenue of research: the Joneses, before we chase up the cars.'

Claire Hannah née Appleton, naturally addressed as 'T' at school, and her husband Edwin Jones rented a cottage in the village of Martley, to the north-west of Worcester in the Teme valley: a country of ancient yews and moss-grown church-yards, half-timbered houses and rural crafts. They rented because they had never scraped enough money together to offer a mortgage company a viable deposit. Edwin's characteristic weakness was sloth, Horace's 'wicked siren'. His intentions, however honourable and praiseworthy, never ventured beyond the gaming table or the tavern counter, and his long-suffering wife despaired of rearing two innocent children in the ways of God. His job, when he had one, was cabinetmaking for the Kidderminster firm of Ingleton & Sowerby, which was so used to his absence, after benders or through his malingering disposition, that it no longer attracted attention. The firm tolerated his behaviour, partly because he was accomplished, and partly because they paid him for his presence but not for his absence. At the time of Wickfield's and Spooner's visit, he had notched up fifty-five winters, the years apparent only too clearly in his drink-sodden face which had once been clean and agreeable, the intoxicating liquor consumed in considerable quantities apparent only too clearly in his heavy paunch. After school he had been successfully apprenticed to a master cabinetmaker and had embraced his new trade with enthusiasm, only to fail to throw off the shackles of his constitutional inertia that prevented any great advancement in his chosen career. Perhaps Claire had had hopes, when she first walked out with the well-favoured and gregarious artificer, of moulding him to more conventional ways, but if so, she failed. At the time of the events unfolded in this chronicle, he was of average height, too stout for his good health, clean-shaven, a smoker of pipes, and in general aspect seedy.

His wife, who had seen fifty-three summers, had the Appleton features of a broad brow, a snub nose and full lips. She practised physiotherapy in the city. By nature she was timid, anxious to please, ingratiating, and Edwin was probably the worst kind of husband to compensate for her lack of confidence: he simply went his own way and could not be steered. Their children, now in their twenties, had flown the nest, and after her day's work was done, Claire could be found at home pottering in the garden, working at her crochet, reading, watching television to while away the hours of her husband's absences in public houses. Outsiders felt sorry for her, but, since a stronger woman would not have permitted her spouse to indulge so frequently and so deeply in the fruits of the vine and the hop, she was to some extent the authoress of her own failure to flourish socially and financially.

After five years of marriage, when the children were still in their infancy, Edwin's fancy was taken by a chance acquaintance who rejoiced in the name of Canubia Walters, and, disdainful of his duties as a husband and father, he flitted one day to cohabit with this curvesome and attractive creature. She, however, being of sterner mettle than her predecessor, would not tolerate his waywardness and lack of personal discipline, and, twelve months after his departure from the family home in Martley, he returned crestfallen, sought forgiveness and was reinstated as master of the household as heretofore. The family's sole external help at this time came from the minister of the Baptist chapel in Worcester, who had heard of the family's troubles from a Martley neighbour of the Joneses who was a parishioner of his and called to see whether he could be of assistance. Claire and Edwin were so impressed with this selfless pastoral call that they took instruction and were in due course accepted as full members of the Baptist church. Little by little their initial appetite for religious observance wavered, but they still proudly considered themselves more or less practising Baptists.

Miriam and Leonard Appleton disapproved of young Edwin. Claire was harmless: ineffective but harmless. One could not really actively dislike her. Edwin, on the other hand, was bumptious as well as indolent, and Leonard took a dislike to his brother-in-law. His view was that Claire had made a mistake in her marriage and would live to regret it. He also considered, albeit concealing the fact from himself because he was not naturally class-conscious, that Claire had married beneath her. The result was that the Appletons and the Joneses saw little of each other, on the level of either generation. Young Rachel knew her aunt Claire only remotely. The latter's children knew their uncle Leonard hardly at all when he died.

Wickfield was anxious to make progress in a case that was proving increasingly opaque: the more information he accumulated, the less clear the matter became. He approached the Joneses, therefore, with less than his usual longanimity; but he had a feeling deep in his bones that something dramatic was about to happen and that the case was drawing to an end. *Utinam.*

He and Spooner motored out to Martley first thing on the Wednesday morning, with Edwin's work address in their pocket in case he should not be at home. One way or the other they would beard him - this was Wickfield's less than fortunate expression, betraying his exasperation – and beard him they did. He was, as Wickfield put it to himself, 'loafing' about the house in pyjamas and dressing-gown, looking less than alert. His hair was uncombed, his cheeks unshaven, the whole less than wholesome. He was eventually prevailed on to produce a pot of coffee, which Wickfield hoped would help sober the man up and introduce a serious and business-like tone into the encounter.

After mutual pleasantries, as Wickfield tried to establish a reasonably civilised atmosphere in which the three men could engage with success in a coherent conversation, Wickfield introduced the main theme.

'Mr Jones,' he said, 'we are investigating the murder of your niece Rachel, and we are coupling that provisionally with the murder of your brother-in-law Leonard in 1951, because we think the two may be connected. The police record at the time shows that you were interviewed in connexion with Leonard's death. Would you like just to run over your testimony again?'

Edwin looked at him with reasonable glimmerings of intelligence, although his scruffy appearance rendered deep thought unlikely.

'It's all in the record, I suppose, Inspector. Need we go over it all again?'

'Yes, please. It will establish a basis for our discussion.'

'Have a heart, Inspector. I'm just not together.'

'Come on, Sir, you're not making things easy for yourself or for us. What were you able to tell the police about the night of Leonard's death?'

'Nothing. I was at home, miles away.'

'Were you able to prove it?'

'Why do I need to prove it? What possible motive could I have for wanting Len dead? I hardly knew the man.'

'I noticed on the door-bell as we came in that your middle initial is R, Sir. What does it stand for?'

'For crying out loud, Inspector, what's that got to do with anything?'

'Just answer the question, please: what does the R stand for?'

'It stands for Richard, but I can't see how that's relevant. Ah, wait a minute, I know: the police at the time were looking for a Mick, weren't they? I remember Sarah telling me that; she got it from the child; and you think a Rick will do just as well! Well, you're quite wrong, Inspector. In fact, you couldn't be wronger. I've never used my middle name: it's just for decoration. I'll tell you what, though: the police made a pig's-ear of the investigation! How difficult could it have been to find an ex-bankrupt Mick amongst Len Appleton's acquaintances? I ask you!'

There was a sudden silence.

'An ex-bankrupt, you say?' Wickfield asked at length. 'How do you know Leonard Appleton's visitor was an ex-bankrupt?'

'Because, well, because Rachel said so. It was one of the things she overheard.'

'No, it wasn't,' retorted Wickfield. 'The only thing she could remember of the conversation was the name Mick. At five years old she wouldn't have known the word "bankrupt" anyway.'

'Well, perhaps she told Sarah and then forgot. I know I got it from somewhere.'

There was another awkward silence as the parties digested this last comment.

'Mr Jones,' Wickfield said slowly. 'I'm beginning to think you know more of this matter than you've told us so far.'

'No, how can I? I was at home reading a book.'

'Can your wife confirm that?'

'Hardly: I wasn't married at the time, but you can't seriously suspect me. I'm out of the picture, Inspector.'

'I'm sorry, Sir, you're not, and every remark you make raises more suspicion in my mind. Let's start from the beginning, and you can tell me all you know.'

Jones sat there, looking less than lively. That morning he was clearly not on best form. He rose from his chair, asking for permission to make himself another coffee and offering to do the same for his visitors. When he returned, he had also combed his hair and had a wash, however desultory, and his manner was slightly more alert.

'If I tell you what I know, Gentlemen, you're not to jump to conclusions. I wasn't directly involved, and you can't make out that I was. In 1951, at the time of Len's death, I was engaged to Claire. We got married six months after – after the, er, event. I had finished my apprenticeship as a cabinetmaker, and I was looking for work. I had met Len on several occasions, and he once dropped into the conversation that he fancied a new wooden settle in his hall. That remark came back to me, and I went over one evening to see him about it. I arrived about nine o'clock, I suppose, and he offered me a drink. He told me he was expecting another friend to call on a private matter at about half-past nine, and he hoped I shouldn't mind getting through my business before then. We chatted about this and that, our wedding plans, his worries about young Rachel being brought up without a mother, that sort of thing, and when the doorbell rang I had only just broached the subject of the settle. "Look," he says, "would you mind disappearing into the kitchen for ten minutes, and then we'll talk about the settle? You'll find today's newspaper out there." What could I say? I did exactly as I was told and disappeared into the kitchen. Ten minutes or so passed, and then I heard voices raised in anger. I stopped reading the paper in order to listen. I could hardly help listening, as the argument was getting more and more animated and drifted clearly enough through into the kitchen. There was a sudden silence, and then I heard the front-door bang. I didn't know quite what to do, so I waited a bit, and then returned to the sitting-room to resume my conversation with Len. He was lying on the floor, with Rachel clinging to the body. There was absolutely nothing I could do, so I scarpered, quick. And that's it.'

'That's not it at all, Mr Jones,' said Wickfield. 'Why on earth didn't you tell the police that you were on the premises at the time of Mr Appleton's murder? You could have given very valuable help.'

'Because I'm not stupid, that's why, Inspector. It was known that Len thought I was an unsuitable match for his sister. I was lazy, I was working class, I was penniless. He was doing his best to have the engagement broken off. Who would have believed me if I said I'd gone to see him about a settle? I had no alibi – I didn't need one, did I, just to see my future brother-in-law about a piece of furniture? – so I thought the best thing to do was to stay out of it altogether. I didn't know anything anyway. I didn't know who Len's visitor could be, or what it was all about, apart from being a request for a loan. Sarah told me all about the police investigation, and there was nothing solid I could have offered.'

'Right, two things, Mr Jones. Do you agree with Rachel that Mr Appleton called his visitor "Mick"?'

'Yes, he said something like, "I'm not being bullied into any scheme, Mick".'

'And that couldn't have been Dick, Rick, Nick or Vic?'

'No, I don't think so. Well, at the time I thought Len said "Mick", and that's what's stuck in my mind.'

'And what was said about bankruptcy?'

'Mick said that, because he had been declared bankrupt, no one would lend him money and that therefore Appleton was his only recourse.'

'I see. But of course you realise, Mr Jones, that that clue is now probably worthless, because records of bankruptcy are wiped out six years after discharge.'

Edwin Jones said nothing.

'Let's come on to Rachel's murder, if we may. Can you account for your whereabouts on Tuesday afternoon of last week, between, say, four o'clock and six o'clock?'

'For heaven's sake, Inspector, you're not trying to pin that on me as well, are you? She was my niece! Family! Who do you think I am?'

'Nevertheless, Mr Jones, you'll have to tell us where you were. Have a think.'

'At work, I suppose. Why wouldn't I be at work?'

'Well, we can easily check up on that. What time would you have finished work?'

'Not before five. And I'd have been at Kidderminster, remember, quite some way from Evesham.'

'And what time does your wife usually get home from work?'

'No fixed time, Inspector. You'll have to ask her yourself about last Tuesday, I'm afraid: I can't remember.'

The interview came to an end. Wickfield sat in the passenger seat as Spooner drove back to the station. There was silence until Wickfield said,

'Well, Sergeant, what are your impressions?'

'Impressions, Sir? Not favourable, I'm afraid. I was thinking that if he was not at work last Tuesday, he could easily have murdered Rachel and fitted into all we know about her death.'

'Go on, I'm listening.'

'Right, this is how it could have been. Our Edwin murdered Len Appleton because he feared that Len would persuade his sister to break off the engagement. Edwin wanted money there and then, to set up a business, and he also wanted to marry Claire, who had more money than he did and would raise him socially with no effort of his own expended. He then realises, through Sarah, that the child Rachel has overheard a crucial piece of evidence, has remembered it for years and years and then acted on it. OK, she got the wrong man, but sooner or later she would meet Edwin again and then remember properly. She had to be eliminated. On one of his days off, or taking time off, he goes down to Evesham to see how far she's got in her process of revenge. He recognises her through photographs, or perhaps in the flesh, and she shows by her remarks, or demeanour, or attitude, that she is beginning to have second thoughts and that perhaps Edwin is her man after all. By that time, she has disclosed her plan to frame Napier. He allows her to carry it through, because it seems happily to implicate Napier and provide the police with an irresistible scapegoat, and then bumps her off. His wife is not to know that he wasn't at home all the while, recovering from a severe attack of crapulence.'

'Hm, I wonder,' Wickfield commented, non-committally. 'I see things wrong with that reconstruction. For example, where did the real Browning come from: did Jones take it down to Evesham with him? Hardly!'

'Well, Sir, we have only Andy's word for it that the gun used in the hold-up was a fake. I think it was a real gun.'

'And how did Jones get Rachel's body to the Baptist chapel?'

'Easy: he had a car. He pretends to help Rachel frame Napier by driving her to Napier's house and keeping cave. Once they're parked outside, he kills her, uses her key to plant the evidence, drives to Cowl Street and dumps the body. He then goes home, leaving Napier as the prime suspect. Nobody's seen him, Edwin – nobody who knows him, anyway – and he's in the clear. As regards Appleton's murder, it wasn't "Mick" that Rachel overheard but "Rick", and the police at the time didn't pick up on Edwin Jones because he wasn't normally known as anything but Edwin.'

'Right, we're going to check up on his story. There's probably not much we can do about his account of Appleton's death, but last week is surely not beyond us. Our first call is his wife at the Worcestershire Royal. Let's hope Jones hasn't got to her first.'

Parking at the hospital was a problem, which they solved by occupying the space reserved for a consultant which happened to be vacant. At reception they were steered to the physiotherapy department, and there, after a little delay, they were introduced to Mrs Jones. Wickfield explained their business in his most soothing manner and invited her to remember back to Tuesday of the previous week. There was no trouble, he assured her: it was merely a routine inquiry.

'What time did you get home that evening, Mrs Jones?'

Mrs Jones was an attractive woman in her fifties, with a round face and large, round, grey-green eyes. The Appleton snub nose and full lips seemed perfectly to complement her other features. Her hair was worn short. She naturally wore a white uniform.

'Tuesday of last week?' she asked. 'Let me see. About six, I think. Just let me check the diary.' After perusal of this invaluable document, she confirmed her previous estimate. 'Yes, the last patient I saw was at five. Finish half five. Home for six. Does that help?'

'Was your husband there when you got home?'

'Ah, that's a trickier question, Inspector. Hold on, let me think. Yes, I think he'd just got in. That's right, we were going out, so ate at six thirty, and he helped me by peeling some vegetables. I remember his saying I hadn't even given him time to look at the post.'

'Thank you, Mrs Jones, that's most helpful. We'll let you get on.'

The two detectives returned to the station, and Wickfield asked his assistant, as they sat in the office, whether he thought they had a case against Edwin Jones.

'A case, Sir? For Leonard's murder, Rachel's, or both?'

'Both. Let's not be niggardly.'

'Right, Leonard's first. He had motive: he told us himself he feared that Appleton was trying to break off the engagement between him and Appleton's younger sister; this could have meant financial disaster. He had opportunity: on his own confession, he was on the spot at the exact time of the murder. Furthermore, his middle name is Richard. As far as Rachel's murder is concerned, a single phone-call will establish whether or not he was at work that day – '

'OK,' Wickfield interrupted. 'Let's make it.'

They broke off their conference while Spooner put a call through to the works manager at Ingleton & Sowerby, cabinetmakers, of Kidderminster, and a few seconds sufficed to establish the fact that Mr Edwin Jones had not been at work on the Tuesday in question. Spooner spun round on his chair to face his chief.

'Right, Sir, that's making it look rather sinister for our Edwin. We know Edwin was at home for six, or thereabouts, and it would have taken him a good half hour to drive from Evesham back home – more likely forty minutes. That still gives him ample time to meet Rachel, say, soon after a quarter past four, go with her to Napier's house, allow her to plant the evidence, murder her in his car, deposit the body behind the chapel and head for home by twenty past five. So he had opportunity. Did he have motive?'

As he here paused, Wickfield spoke. 'Well, did he?' he asked.

'I'm not sure, Sir. We've already suggested he did, but you pointed out some flaws in our argument. He had motive to murder Rachel only if he were responsible for her father's death; otherwise Rachel was no threat to him. On the other hand, no other suspect stands out as looking quite so likely as our Edwin.'

The two men reviewed the evidence against Mr Jones, taking into account the various strands of the case, and came to the conclusion that, despite gaps, it would persuade a jury to bring in a verdict of guilty. Edwin Jones was arrested on a double charge of murder and remanded in custody, loudly protesting his innocence and calling down imprecations on the police.

Thirteen

Six months later, the case was heard at Worcester Crown Court before judge (Mr Justice Charles Oddsman) and jury, counsel being Mr Francis Potts for the prosecution and Mr Graeme Mackenzie for the defence. It was a muggy day in late June, and the windows of the court-room stood open to admit the slightest breeze. The jury were sworn in – five women and seven men – and amid considerable publicity the trial began. The defendant, sitting composedly in the dock, wore blue jeans and an open-neck check shirt. Counsel for the prosecution rose to inaugurate the main proceedings.

'Your Honour, members of the jury, the case before you today is an unusual one, in that the defendant is accused of two related murders committed twenty years apart but connected by family and by motive. The first murder was committed on 3 February 1951, in a house on the outskirts of Evesham. The Crown's case is that the defendant, Edwin Jones, paid a visit one evening to his future brother-in-law to ask for a loan for a business he intended to set up. He was short of money because of gambling debts, but he had promised his fiancée to turn over a new leaf, and his future happiness depended on funds being forthcoming. His request was refused, and, losing his temper, he throttled Leonard Appleton to death. He was unaware that his victim's daughter, Rachel, who was five years old at the time, had overheard at least part of his conversation with Mr Appleton and had remembered the address "Mick". The Crown contends that that was a child's easily intelligible mistake for "Rick". This item of information the defendant later learnt from his sister-in-law - his new wife's sister and Rachel's aunt -

who brought Rachel up as her own daughter. However, for the moment no danger threatened, and he began to think that he had got away with murder.

'However, twenty years later, he learnt, again through his sister-in-law, that Rachel, overhearing a man in a pub and, wrongly identifying him as her father's killer, intended to frame him for a series of crimes that carried a custodial sentence. The defendant, who occasionally saw his wife's niece, began to be afraid that Rachel would realise her mistake and correctly identify the defendant. To pre-empt this, he took steps to make contact with Rachel, one day in January of this year. He met her in Evesham, as she was leaving home coincidentally to plant evidence on her victim. He gave her a lift, accompanied her to her victim's house, shot her in the chest, drove a little way across the town to the Baptist chapel, hid the body there and returned home.

'I shall be calling witnesses to prove that Rachel Carver had been in his car, that he had access to the murder weapon, that he lied to police in claiming to be at work at the time of her murder. Of course, Your Honour and members of the jury, I cannot produce photographs of the defendant shooting his niece or hiding the body, but you will agree with me that the evidence for his guilt accumulated by the Crown in an exhaustive inquiry is compelling. I should also wish to state that the location of Mrs Carver's murder is not part of the Crown's case. I do not wish to be specific as to where – in a house, or in a car, or in the street – she was murdered.'

The first witness for the prosecution was Detective Inspector Stanley Wickfield. He was duly called. He stumbled as he mounted the witness-box. The favourable impression created by his kindly and intelligent physiognomy was to some extent damaged by the strange way in which he wore his clothes, even when he had brushed them down and arranged his features into a suitably serious and sombre expression.

'Inspector, would you outline to the Court the steps you took before taking the defendant into custody?'

'Yes, I can do that. At the start of the investigation, we kept an open mind as to whether Mrs Carver's murder was the result of a random killing, for example, for motives of theft or sexual assault, or whether, rather, it was somehow connected with her father's death of twenty years before. We simultaneously ruled out the former and established the latter. Mrs Carver's husband told us that his wife had been engaged in a vendetta against a certain citizen of Evesham on the basis that she had recognised his voice from twenty years previously as that of her father's killer. Our investigation led us to conclude that the man she had picked on, although he was a Michael, was quite innocent, and other leads came to nothing. We therefore widened our inquiry, and the evidence against the defendant appeared increasingly cogent.'

'Why did you not suspect the defendant in the first stages of your inquiry?'

'Two things, really. One was that the defendant was not Michael, or Nicholas, or Victor, or any other name that could have been shortened to an -ick sound. I should perhaps explain to the Court that Rachel Carver was convinced that she remembered her father addressing his evening visitor as "Mick". It was suggested at the time of original inquiry that she could have misheard Dick, Nick, Rick or Vic.'

'Yes, I've already mentioned this, Inspector.'

'Oh, sorry. Well, we had kept an open mind on that, but we first of all explored associates of Mr Appleton whose names could have been so heard before looking more widely. It was only then that we discovered that the defendant's middle name was Richard.'

There was an audible and satisfied gasp from the courtroom.

'The second thing was that the defendant and his wife seem not to have been close to the rest of the family, except perhaps latterly, and the original investigating team had only a tenuous reason to interview him. It was really not until we came to look more closely at his alibis for both murders and at possible motives that his actions and prevarications began to be suspicious.'

'Will you tell the Court what alibis the defendant offered?'

'For Len Appleton's murder, the defendant admits to being in the house and to overhearing the quarrel between the deceased and his killer. It is our contention that the defendant was himself the killer. For Rachel Carver's murder, the defendant originally claimed to have been at work, but our inquiries showed that he was not at work, nor was he at home. In a word, he has no alibi.'

At the conclusion of his testimony, in which he outlined the police reconstruction of the events with Edwin Jones at their centre, the counsel for the defence rose to cross-examine.

'Inspector Wickfield,' Mr Mackenzie began, 'I understand from my client that when you first interviewed him at home, he was not cautioned. Is that correct?'

'Yes, I'm afraid it's correct. You see – '

'No, no, Inspector, you've answered my question. It follows that none of his comments is admissible in this court.'

When Wickfield did not reply, counsel said, 'Doesn't it?'

'Yes,' Wickfield said unhappily.

'Then we shall just have to wait for my client to give testimony on his own behalf. At this stage we have no reason to doubt that the defendant's account of his actions is perfectly proper and does not implicate him in any way. My second question is this: have you any reason to believe that the defendant was ever known to Mr Appleton, or indeed to anyone else, as "Rick"?'

'Er, no.'

'Why is his middle name relevant, in that case?'

'It isn't. I should explain to you that we also worked on the hypothesis that the child Rachel misheard the conversation completely, and that what she mistook for "Mick" was some completely innocuous word like brick or stick.'

'It seems to me, Inspector, that you were trying to persuade the Court that the defendant's middle name somehow implies guilt. You now admit that it is completely irrelevant. It could be Mahershalalhashbaz or Nebuchadnezzar for all the relevance it has.' There were titters in the court-room.

'That may be so, but there is other evidence against the defendant.'

'We shall hear that in due course, I dare say,' counsel said, 'but if it's anything like yours, it will not harm my client unduly.'

The judge at his bench erupted in displeasure at this remark, and counsel hastily withdrew it, but not, of course, before it had influenced the jury.

The second witness for the prosecution was the owner of a gun-shop in Worcester, a Mr Absalom Pearl.

'Mr Pearl,' Mr Potts said ingratiatingly, as he handed a clear plastic wallet to the witness, 'would you look at this gun, please? Does the serial number match any with which you are familiar?'

'Yes, Sir, it does.'

'Would you tell the Court about it, please?'

'The serial number on this gun is T135-489. According to my records, I sold that gun to a Mr Edwin R. Jones on 3 April 1964.'

'Would you just confirm for the Court what kind and model of gun it is?'

'Of course. It is a 9 mm Browning Hi-Power semi-automatic, single-action, recoil operated pistol, using a 13-round staggered magazine and – '

'Yes, thank you, Mr Pearl, I think the Court is satisfied.'

The third witness for the prosecution was a ballistics expert, a certain Mr Jabez Bunting.

'Mr Bunting,' said Mr Potts, as he handed the same plastic envelope up to the witness-stand, 'could you confirm that this is the gun you examined at the request of Detective Inspector Wickfield, of Worcester CID, in connexion with the death of Mrs Rachel Carver in January of this year?'

Mr Bunting turned it this way and that, read the serial number of the gun contained in the bag, compared it with the number written on a piece of paper taken from his jacket pocket, and replied affirmatively.

'Would you tell the Court whether, in your opinion, the bullets removed from Mrs Carver's chest were fired by this gun?'

'Yes, certainly, there can be no doubt.'

'Would you just explain to the jury how you can be so sure?'

'Well, it's quite simple. I took the gun, fired it into a box of gel and then compared the marks of the bullet, under a microscope, with the marks on the bullets that killed Mrs Carver. It is to some extent a pity that no cartridge-cases were available for comparison, but they would not have made any real difference. The bullet-marks already matched in every detail.'

'And there is no doubt in your mind?'

'None whatever.'

'Thank you, Mr Bunting, you may stand down.'

Next the prosecution called for a Mr Nigel Wetherton to take the witness-stand. After taking an oath to tell the truth, he began by affirming his identity.

'Mr Wetherton, do you work for the Forensic Science Service?'

'I do.'

'Is your speciality the inspection of cars for evidence of a person's presence in the car?'

'It's part of my work, yes.'

'Would you tell the court what you found in the defendant's car?'

'I was asked to look for traces of Mrs Rachel Carver. The search was hampered by the fact that the car had been recently vacuumed, but I recovered a number of hairs which were positively identified as belonging to Mrs Carver.'

'Can you think of any way in which these hairs could have got there if Mrs Carver had not been in the car?'

'That's a bit of a funny question, if I may say so -- with respect, of course. The answer is that Mrs Carver's presence in the car is the most obvious explanation, but I cannot rule out that hairs on, say, the driver's coat fell off in the course of travel, or that Mrs Carver's own coat had been put on the passenger seat at some stage.'

The counsel for the defence came to his feet to cross-examine.

'Whereabouts in the car did you discover Mrs Carver's hairs, Mr Wetherton?'

'They were in the compartment occupied by the front passenger.'

'Was there any evidence that her body had been carried in the boot?'

'No, none.'

'Or in the back?'

'No.'

'Were you asked also to look for evidence that a pistol had been fired at close range in the car?'

'I was.'

'And what was the result of your search?'

'I found nothing.'

'Would you have expected to find something?'

He hesitated before replying. 'It's difficult to say,' he eventually told the Court. 'If the car had been examined immediately, I should have expected to find some powder adhering to the dash-board or foot-mat or upholstery, but too much time elapsed, and I was not surprised to find nothing.'

'Thank you, Mr Bunting.'

However, as the witness made to stand down, counsel for the prosecution indicated his desire to ask a further question.

'Mr Bunting, could Mrs Carver's body have been carried in the boot without leaving any trace?'

'Mm, probably.'

'How?'

'Well, for example if it had been sealed in a heavy-duty black plastic bag.'

'Thank you, Mr Bunting. That's all I wished to ask.'

The next witness for the prosecution was Mrs Platt, Rachel Carver's aunt and substitute mother.

'Mrs Platt,' Mr Potts said with confidence, aware that his case was proceeding according to plan, 'would you tell the Court about your brother Len's opinion of the defendant?'

The witness was plainly ill at ease.

'Can I say at once,' she said, 'that personally I like the defendant?'

'No, Mrs Platt, please answer the question: that's all you need do.'

'Very well, but I wish to make it clear that I am testifying against my will.'

'Will the witness please answer the question,' the judge said severely.

'Yes, Your Honour, if I have to. Len didn't like the defendant.' When she stopped abruptly, counsel urged her to expand on her statement.

'It was nothing really to do with Len, but he felt a certain responsibility for his sister, because he knew her to be, shall we say, easily swayed. He got to know the defendant on a couple of family occasions and took a dislike to him.'

'For what reasons, Mrs Platt?'

'He thought Edwin was shallow, a playboy. He thought he would never keep a job down, that he gambled and drank too much, and – ' She hesitated.

'Yes, Mrs Platt?'

' – that he was working class. I know that's what he thought, even though he didn't say so in as many words. He was concerned for Claire: he thought her fiancé an unsuitable match from every point of view.'

'And if he succeeded in breaking off the engagement, what would have been the financial consequences for the defendant?'

'Objection, Your Honour. My learned friend is inviting the witness to speculate and surmise.'

'Objection overruled. The witness may answer the question.'

'Please, Your Honour,' the witness said, turning directly to the judge, 'I never had any long discussions with my brother on this matter. I may be making things up.'

'Just tell the Court what your brother actually said, if he said anything relevant,' the judge said. 'You're quite right that we want only the facts.'

Somewhat mollified, Mrs Platt resumed her comments. 'My brother said that Edwin Jones was a gold-digger and that he should have no Appleton money. But it wasn't true, Your Honour.'

'What wasn't true, Mrs Platt?' This was Mr Potts.

'It wasn't true that Edwin was a gold-digger. He was a nice young man, and Len was prejudiced, that's all.'

Mr Potts was unhappy with the witness's testimony, but there was nothing he could now do to correct it. Perhaps no damage had been done.

The defence case rested on one character witness and on the testimony of the defendant himself.

'Mr Darlington, are you the managing director of Ingleton & Sowerby, cabinetmakers, of Kidderminster?'

'I am.'

'How long has the defendant been working for you?'

'A long time. Over twenty years, anyway.'

'Would you give us an honest assessment of the defendant's character?'

'Let me be quite frank with the Court. Edwin Jones makes life difficult for us, because of his absences. My understanding is that alcohol plays a major part in this. I should like to add, however, that he is a perfectly charming and amiable person in himself, and that I have never had the slightest cause to doubt his honesty or integrity.'

'Has he ever demonstrated violence or loss of temper at work?'

'No, never, as far as I know.'

'Would you consider him capable of murder?'

'Objection, Your Honour.'

'Objection sustained.'

Counsel for the prosecution rose to cross-examine.

'Mr Darlington, you are managing director of the firm?'

'Yes.'

'How much time does that position allow you to spend on the shop floor?'

'Not nearly so much as I should like. You see, these days – '

'Yes, thank you, Mr Darlington, please confine yourself to the questions asked. Do you know the defendant very well?'

'Well, not intimately, if that's what you mean. I'm mean, we're not friends in the accepted sense of that word.'

'Have you ever been to his house?'

'No.'

'Has he ever been to yours?'

'No.'

'Are you really in a position to give a rounded character reference?'

'Well, I can say only how the defendant strikes me.'

'Thank you, Mr Darlington.'

It was then the defendant's turn to climb into the witness-box.

'Mr Jones,' his defence counsel said, 'you have chosen to testify under oath in your own behalf. I'm going to take you through the two cases for which you stand charged, and you are to give the Court truthful answers. Let us begin with the more recent murder, that of Mrs Carver. Would you first of all tell the Court what you know of the Browning Hi-Power that was used to kill the unfortunate Mrs

133

Carver? We have heard from a prosecution witness that it was your gun.'

'Certainly. Yes, I bought the gun in 1964 for target practice. It was stolen in a burglary at our house in 1968. I mentioned it to the police at the time. Since then, of course, it could have been sold on any number of times. I haven't seen it for years.'

'Would you now tell the Court where you were at the time of Rachel's death?'

'And when was that?'

'Tuesday 12 January, between the hours of four fifteen and five forty-five.'

'I can't remember.'

'Well, I think I can assist you there, Mr Jones. You initially told the police you were at work, but they found out that you weren't. I suggest that you were frightened to admit to the police that you were illegally drinking in a public house – '

'Objection, Your Honour. Counsel is putting words into the defendant's mouth.'

'Objection sustained. Mr Mackenzie, you must let the defendant answer for himself.'

'Yes, Your Honour. I was only trying – '

'I know what you were trying to do. Please allow the defendant to speak entirely for himself.'

'Right, Your Honour. So let's get back to your whereabouts at the time of Rachel's death. Where were you, Mr Jones?'

'I was in a public house.'

'Were there any witnesses?'

'Yes, of course, I'd hardly be drinking on my own.' There were one or two titters in the court-room.

'How long were you there?'

'An hour or more, probably.'

'From when till when?'

'Probably half four to six, something like that.'

'Thank you, Mr Jones. Would you now explain to the Court why some of Mrs Carver's hairs might have been found in your car?'

'Yes, certainly, there's no mystery there. Rachel Carver was my niece, by marriage. I didn't see her very often, but I had known her almost from infancy. Very occasionally we met for a coffee, usually in Worcester, but sometimes in Evesham if I was in the locality. I'd give her a ring and say, Fancy a coffee this morning?, and we'd meet and chat. Rachel didn't have any class prejudices, you see.' He made a meaningful pause. 'The latest occasion was some time last autumn, when we met in Worcester on her day off.'

'Right, thank you. I want now to revert to the events surrounding the death of Mr Leonard Appleton twenty years ago, for which you also stand charged. Would you tell the Court what you were doing in Leonard Appleton's house on the night he was murdered?'

'I'd gone round to see whether he was serious about having a piece of hall furniture made. I was trying to set myself up as a cabinetmaker, and he had made some mention of a hall-seat.'

'Please tell the Court what happened.'

'I was talking to Len - my future brother-in-law - when there was a ring at the doorbell. Len said he had arranged to see a friend, would I excuse him for ten minutes, so I disappeared into the kitchen. I heard an argument going on in the sitting-room, and the next thing I knew, the visitor slammed the front-door. I returned to the sitting-room to find Len dead on the floor.'

'And why didn't you phone the police?'

'Because I didn't think they'd believe my story. I went home as fast as I could.'

'Had you any means of identifying the assailant?'

'No, I never saw him.'

'I understand you overheard some of the conversation between Mr Appleton and his visitor. Please tell the Court what you heard.'

'Well, I didn't hear much, because I was in the kitchen, you see, as I've already said. I heard only a bit when the voices were raised. Len called his visitor "Mick" – I'm fairly sure it was Mick – and something was said about a loan or the visitor would be in trouble. That's all.'

'Did you know Rachel was in the house?'

'Well, yes, of course she was in the house, but I didn't know at the time that she'd heard any of the conversation, if that's what you mean.'

'How did you know?'

'How did I know what?'

'That Rachel had overheard some of the conversation.'

'Because Sarah – that's Mrs Platt, Rachel's aunt – told me.'

'Did Mrs Platt think that Rachel had got the wrong man?'

'I don't know: she never said.'

'What did you think?'

'I trusted Rachel's judgement.'

'So why didn't you go to the police at that point?'

'Because I had no proof. The police weren't going to listen to some cock-and-bull story about a five-year-old girl hearing a voice and remembering it twenty years later. What could I tell them? I should certainly never have recognised the voice myself.'

'Would Rachel have recognised your voice if you'd been the visitor, do you think?'

'Of course. She knew me well enough, even though I wasn't yet married to her aunt.'

'How did she address you?'

'As Mr Jones.'

'Could she have got confused about Mick and your voice, when she knew you as Mr Jones? What if her father had said "Rick", but because she didn't know you as Rick, she didn't make the connexion?'

'No, of course not. Len Appleton never called me Rick anyway.'

Mr Potts for the prosecution cross-examined the defendant.

'Mr Jones, some might say that your action, running from the house without informing the police, was that of a guilty man.'

'But I wasn't guilty.'

'Had you no concern for your little niece, left alone in the house with her father lying dead?'

'I panicked. I couldn't think straight. All I could think was that the police wouldn't believe me and that I would do best to get out as fast as I could.'

'Did you have money troubles at that time?'

'Not to say "troubles", exactly. Money was always a bit tight, you know. I was only just starting out in business; and I was saving to get married.'

'Then why do you imagine that Mr Appleton thought you were a gold-digger?'

'Because he didn't like me. Prejudice.'

'I put it to you, Mr Jones, that it was you who strangled Mr Appleton because he wouldn't lend you money, you disliked him, you lost your temper. It's as simple as that.'

'That's not true,' Jones almost shouted. 'I had nothing to do with his death, and you can't prove I did.'

'All right. Let me now come to Rachel Carver's death, Mr Jones. You admit she was in your car last autumn. You also admit that you and she did not meet very often. Isn't it a bit of a coincidence that you arranged to see her at about the same time as she met her death?'

'I can't help coincidences, can I?'

'Did you know that she was pursuing a completely innocent businessman because she mistakenly believed he was her father's killer?'

'I knew she was pursuing someone, but how do I know whether he was the right guy or not?'

'Where did you hear it from?'

Edwin looked at the judge, for guidance. The latter waved a hand as if to indicate that he could safely answer the question.

'From my sister-in-law Sarah.'

'Did you think that sooner or later Rachel would realise her mistake and cotton on to you instead?'

'Objection, Your Honour! Counsel is trying to get the defendant to incriminate himself.'

'Objection sustained. Please carry on, Mr Potts, but you mustn't ask the defendant questions which he can't answer truthfully without incriminating himself.'

'Mr Jones, don't you think it's a massive coincidence that, out of hundreds, thousands, of pistols in circulation, it was yours that was used to kill Mrs Carver? Doesn't that seem extraordinary to you?'

'No, not really. If my gun was stolen by a local man – or woman, of course - ' he added with a snigger, 'and sold locally, it would still be around Worcestershire, wouldn't it?'

'I have no more questions, Your Honour.'

Mr Mackenzie then summed up for the defence.

'Your Honour, Members of the Jury, my client is charged with two counts of murder, but I submit that neither has been proved. The prosecution argue that Mr Jones' murder of Rachel Carver hinged on motives relating to her father's murder of twenty years earlier. If I can satisfy you that there is no case for my client to answer on the count of that first murder, I submit that the motive for Rachel Carver's murder which my client is alleged to have harboured crashes fatally to the ground.

'I ask you, therefore, whether the prosecution have proved, beyond reasonable doubt, that Mr Jones murdered his future brother-in-law in 1951. There is no doubt whatsoever in my mind that no such proof has been forthcoming, despite my learned friend's best efforts to manufacture evidence where there is none. First of all, my client is said to have approached Mr Appleton for a loan. No proof for this has been offered. Secondly, he is said to have confronted Mr Appleton, to have lost his temper and to have strangled him in fury. My client admits to being in the house at the time, but he has a perfectly acceptable and logical explanation for that, and the prosecution have produced not a scrap of proof to support the allegation of murder. Thirdly, the prosecution have done their best to muddy the waters by giving credence to a child's memory of a Mick and to the defendant's middle name of Richard. This is so flimsy as to be risible, and I urge you solemnly to discount it entirely.

'In short, there is no case against my client for the terrible murder of Mr Leonard Appleton in 1951. Because of that, I contend that my client had absolutely no motive for murdering Mrs Carver, his own niece. I will add, however, for the sake of completion, that the prosecution's case for the murder of Mrs Carver is entirely, but entirely, supposititious. No proof has been offered that the defendant was in Evesham at the time of her death. He has given a perfectly satisfactory account of losing his gun years before the crime and of how Rachel's hair was in his car. You will consequently, members of the jury, bring in a verdict of Not Guilty, I am sure.'

Mr Justice Oddsman summed up, directed the jury on questions of law and dismissed them to consider their verdict. Wickfield and

Spooner took stock in the meantime.

'Well, Sergeant, what think you?'

'I'm afraid I think the defence made a better case, Sir.'

'Yes, I'm rather afraid I agree with you. I think we've been too hasty in assembling a case against Edwin Jones. He may be as guilty as Cain, but there just isn't the evidence.'

It had always puzzled him greatly that king Solomon, endowed with more wisdom than any other mortal, more than Ethan, Heman, Chalcol and Darda, the four sons of Mahol (who was he? wondered Wickfield), still lacked the virtue to abide by his covenant with God. This was all the more noteworthy in that, in the Bible, as Wickfield remembered from many years before, wisdom lay not so much in the intelligence and understanding as in the application of God's law to daily life. Wisdom meant living a life in conformity with virtue. Yet in the present instance, despite his extensive experience in the field of detection, he, Wickfield, had allowed his impatience to override his common sense. He wondered how he could have blundered so painfully; carried away by frustration and impatience, he supposed, but he should not have allowed it.

Four hours elapsed before the jury returned their verdict.

'Members of the jury, are you agreed on your verdict?'

'We are, Your Honour.'

'And what is your verdict?'

'Not guilty, Your Honour.'

Perhaps they would have brought in a verdict of Not Proven, if that had been legally permissible. Wickfield and Spooner would never find out.

Fourteen

Although the verdict was a disappointment and a reversal, Wickfield had the grace to admit that it was largely his own fault. It was not that Edwin Jones was innocent; it was just that the detective team had not accumulated enough sturdy evidence to persuade the jury to bring in a verdict of guilty. The chief inspector, however, knowing less of the case than Wickfield, accepted the court's acquittal and urged him to continue his inquiry.

'Look, Wickfield,' he said, 'you've blundered, and I partly blame myself for letting you. I didn't think you'd need such close supervision at this stage of your career. We've succeeded in making the police a laughing-stock, and we're going to have to clear our name. I shall correct that: *you*'re going to have to clear our name. Get out there and find the real villain. It's not beyond you, I trust. I'm going to give you a week, and after that – well, I don't know what I shall do, but the outlook for you won't be very rosy.'

'No, Sir. I'm sorry, Sir. The case is getting me down. I'm like Daedalus in his labyrinth: I can't find a way out. Or do I mean Theseus, who couldn't find his way in?'

'Stop talking nonsense, Wickfield, and get back out there. Go and find some villains: that's what you're paid for.'

Dispirited, the inspector returned to his office, not knowing quite where to turn next. Although he was still sure that Edwin Jones was guilty, the court-case said otherwise. The trouble was that, in Wickfield's mind, there was no other villain out there; he was not looking for any other suspect in the case. He had it all wrapped up, the facts were catered for, the theory fitted the facts – motive, opportunity, means – so what was left? The tendering of his resignation, perhaps? Not to be contemplated for a moment; well, not for long, anyway.

Fortunately for his mental and emotional equilibrium, Spooner, the faithful and ever-cooperative Spooner, came to his rescue. As Wickfield entered his office, the sergeant rose to his feet and flourished a plastic bag with what, in Spooner, passed for excitement.

'Here we are, Sir: the big break-through!'

'Oh, yes, Sergeant, what is it this time? We thought we had the big break-through with our friend Edwin - may his hair fall out and his knee-caps fester – so you'll perhaps forgive me if I don't launch into a jig.'

'No, Sir, this is the Big One: it's Rachel's handbag!'

'Ah!' was all Wickfield squeezed out between his thin lips, but after a minute, he said, 'How can you be sure it's going to be of any assistance to us?'

Spooner was rather deflated.

'Well, I can't be, of course, Sir, but I thought it might turn up something. It's better than no handbag.'

'Yes, you're right, Sergeant. Don't mind me: I'm just not in a very good mood. So, what's all this about?'

'Well, Sir, it's like this. A woman was out walking her dog – an Alsatian, I believe it was, one of those long-haired ones – '

'Yes, yes, Sergeant, get to the point.'

' – and she was on the footpath that follows the river along Waterside. When she came to the bridge that carries the Cheltenham Road over the river, she noticed this bag caught in a crevice in the stone-work. It was as if somebody had launched it into the void, hoping to hit the water with it, but it hit an obstacle and ricocheted back. Anyway, being a sensible and responsible sort of person – '

'All women are, Sergeant.'

'Yes, Sir - being a sensible and responsible person, she reached it down and handed it in to the police-station. She naturally thought – this is what she told Constable Allerton at the desk this morning – that it would contain keys or papers that its owner would miss. It looked to her as if the owner had accidentally dropped it over the parapet and then thought it lost for ever as it disappeared into the murky waters of the Avon as they flowed sluggishly through the muddy banks on their way to Pershore and thence - '

'Yes, yes, Spooner, what on earth's got into you this morning? Just give me the facts.'

'Those are the facts, Sir. A woman found the handbag this morning, handed it in to the Evesham police, and here it is. Isn't it lovely?'

'Presumably the Evesham station identified it as Rachel's and sent it on here. Right, let's have a good look.'

Donning gloves, the pair shook the handbag out of its plastic cocoon, opened it up and disgorged the contents carefully on to the table. Most of it was the usual contents of a handbag: lipstick and other cosmetics, a handkerchief, a purse, a sewing-kit, a small pair of scissors, some chewing-gum, a packet of mints, and so on. Only one item caught their particular attention: a small sheaf of papers. On inspection, these were seen to be on headed notepaper: Mrs Christine Braithwaite, the caption proudly ran, Registered Hypnotherapist. There followed various letters indicating diplomas, degrees and membership of professional bodies, an address in Worcester and a telephone-number. The papers were full of crossings-out and insertions, as if the writer were struggling to give accurate expression to difficult thoughts. After all the corrected and altered versions came what seemed to Wickfield and Spooner to be a fair copy. They read:

> 'Don't be ridiculous. Have some sense, man, before you say something stupid. I'm not going in with you, and that's final. I can't afford it, for a start, and I think the animal's too frisky. You might want to run her for high stakes, if you like, but I've made the bid I consider appropriate, and I'm not going to put my hard-earned money where I might lose the lot.'

> 'Are you saying I'd be unable to negotiate, because if you are, you'd better be careful. I'll have you know I'm a far cleverer operator than you'll ever be, and if you don't recognise a unique opportunity when you see it, you're a bigger mug than I took you for. I tell you she'll work: she'll make an almighty splash, because she's one helluva piece of horseflesh, and you're a fool not to go in with me.'

'It's not such a clever scheme: you're not being frank. '

'You know damn well I am: you're making me out to be corrupt. Thanks: a crook, me? Don't talk such bull. All you lack is a bit of savvy and a spirit of adventure. Come on, Len, what do you say?'

'No, no, and again no! I'm not to be bullied into buying Dream Chick, and I'd be glad if you'd take your hare-brained plans elsewhere else and leave me in peace. When will you understand that I'm just not interested?'

'I'm off to France for a life-time, where it's nice and sunny. This is the chance I've been waiting for, and you're the only thing in my way.'

'I'm not in your way, not in the least. You go ahead, but it'll have to be without me.'

'Damn you, Len, damn you to hell. It's money for old rope. After all the tears, you reap what you sow.'

'You're nothing but a spendthrift, and I don't mean to put my family at risk. Look, we've talked enough. You'd better go before we fall out.'

'Len, that's really not funny. I'm very upset again. I've pinned my hopes on you, and you've got to help me, fast. I must have that horse.'

'I haven't got to help you at all. She's a handsome roan, but the mount you want does not respond, and in any case I'm not risking it. Now please go away, and let's hear no more about it.'

Baxter.

After concentrated perusal of this strange dialogue, Wickfield was moved to speech.

'Well,' he said, 'it does not require a doctorate in philosophy to deduce what this purports to be. What do you make of it, Spooner, my lad?'

'As you say, Sir, it's obvious. Rachel Carver had been attending sessions of hypnotherapy to clarify her remembrance of the conversation she overheard at five years old between her father and her father's killer. Quite where it leaves us is a different matter.'

'Very cautious, Sergeant, very cautious. I can see you're not going to stick your neck out just yet. Perhaps you and I should have a word with the divine Mrs Braithwaite. This could just be our salvation.'

'Excuse me, Sir, how do you know she's divine?'

'Spooner, my lad, you're in a funny mood today. Are you on something? I'll tell you why she's divine: all women are until you find out otherwise. That's the proper spirit in which to approach members of the opposite sex. Let's be going.'

Mrs Braithwaite occupied a consulting-room in North Parade. A brass plaque on the street announced her qualifications and her hours of attendance, and adjacent stairs led to the first floor where the consultant hypnotherapist awaited them. Mrs Braithwaite was not exactly divine – thought Wickfield; Spooner's assessment is not recorded - but she was homely. Wickfield estimated her age at forty; a rather sharp face but kindly eyes; very neat hair scraped back into a plait. She wore a smart dark suit bearing a silver brooch that depicted a running fox. Her consulting room was bright, open and cheerful. Potted plants and cut flowers stood on ledges and tables. Some easy-chairs, an imposing desk, an office-chair behind it, a bookshelf and – of course! – a couch completed the furniture. The windows, framed by red and green chintz curtains, gave on to the river. Pictures of sea-scapes and a portrait of Sigmund Freud adorned the walls. A door on the opposite side of the room led, Wickfield presumed, to a kitchen and a toilet.

Mrs Braithwaite welcomed the two men fulsomely.

'Gentlemen, such a pleasure! How generous of you to honour my humble rooms! Now I didn't quite gather on the phone what it was about which you wished to consult me: something to do with a former client, was it? And here was I thinking you'd want to drag me in handcuffs down to the station; instead you honour me with a visit. Charmed, I'm sure. Gentlemen, let's not stand on ceremony: please be seated. Coffee? Tea?'

When they had eventually got settled, Wickfield thought he could safely begin without a further torrent of blandiloquence.

'Mrs Braithwaite, we've come about Mrs Rachel Carver, who, we think, must have been a client of yours last year. Perhaps you remember her?'

'Oh, yes, Inspector, I remember her all right: a very interesting case. But you realise I cannot reveal anything about our consultations: that would be quite unprofessional.'

'Did you not know that she was killed in January? There was a court-case about it recently.'

'Good heavens, was that her? I had no idea. Gracious, it's given me quite a turn.' Indeed she looked genuinely perturbed. After a moment or so, Wickfield gave her a few details.

'Thank you, Inspector. I don't generally follow crime in the papers: distasteful and disturbing, not my cup of tea at all. But to think my Rachel was murdered. My word, whatever next? It's a wicked, wicked world, isn't it, Inspector?'

'It is indeed, Mrs Braithwaite. So I take it that your reservations about revealing professional secrets no longer apply? I hope not, because we need your help.'

'Yes, of course, Inspector. I shall be privileged to help if I can. We professional people have a duty to be of assistance to the forces of law and order.'

'Perhaps you could start by telling us how and why Mrs Carver came to consult you.'

'Very well. She came to me in September of last year. She told me about her father's murder, how she had overheard a snatch of conversation, how she had recognised the voice and that she was now debating within herself how best to proceed. You'll know all about that, I daresay. Actually, between you and me, Gentlemen, she wasn't entirely honest with me, as I later discovered. She had already set this man up for a theft on a jeweller's shop and was contemplating further – action, if that is the appropriate word. Of course, I suspected none of that at the time. When I did discover it, I broke off our consultations at once. I was certainly not to be party, even in the remotest way, to any criminal scheme.'

'So what exactly was her reason for coming to you?'

'Well, what she told me was this. She had recognised the voice and wished to go to the police with the identity of the voice's owner. She was fully aware, however, that she had no proof whatever. She hoped, therefore, that I could help her recover a firmer memory of what she had overheard, and that that would give her the evidence she needed to approach the police with a greater chance of success.'

'And were you able to help her?'

'That's a big question, you know. Yes, I was able to help her, but -'

'Ah, I guessed there'd be a but,' Spooner said, 'there always is.'

Mrs Braithwaite gave him a look that could be described as baleful. She resumed with a sniff.

'I was able to help her, and in fact we were doing very well, but then, as I say, I got wind of criminal intent and broke off our relationship. Her memories were returning but were not yet complete.'

Wickfield produced the written sheets taken from Rachel Carver's handbag and handed them solemnly to the hypnotherapist.

'Have you seen these before, Mrs Braithwaite?' he asked.

'Oh, yes, dear, that's what we were working on when we parted company, she and I.'

'Could you just explain a little bit about how you were working to recover her memories? I should like a clearer picture of how reliable her memories might be.'

'Well – I hope you've got time for this, Inspector – and Sergeant too, of course – because this may take a while.'

'Perhaps you could give us an abbreviated account?' Wickfield asked hopefully.

'Very well, but it's really most interesting, you know. I mean, I could go on for a very long time. No, no, I realise that would not meet the present case. Let me just tell you this, then. I am a disciple of Freud. Oh, yes, the very greatest psychoanalyst of them all. He didn't get everything right, by any means, but he laid the foundations of the discipline, you know, and his basic insights have remained unshaken for fifty years: not unchallenged – there are mean spirits in every department of science – but unshaken. Now Freud divided the mind into three. Not three compartments, as it might be of a handbag, you understand, but three functions. First of all, there is conscience, which he called the superego, where all value judgements, intellectual judgements, about the rights and wrongs of one's actions are lodged. These are derived from one's parents and from society. You appreciate, of course, that I'm simplifying absurdly.'

'Please go on, Mrs Braithwaite: quite fascinating.'

'Then there is the ego, the conscious mind, all the things that are going on in your mind at any given time, what you're aware of and can give an account of.'

'Yes, I see,' said Wickfield, out of politeness.

'And finally – and this is his great triumph – he posited the id.' She stopped abruptly, as if contemplating the splendour of this achievement. 'Now ask yourselves, Gentlemen – I'm just going to give you a very crude example; nothing fancy or high-faluting, you understand, just a simple example. Imagine I asked you what you had for last Sunday's lunch. You'd be very unlikely to be able to tell me without thinking about it, but after a bit of thought you could probably remember what you had. Now Freud asked himself, where was that memory when you weren't thinking of it? Where had it disappeared to? His answer was – and why nobody had thought of it before is beyond me – not thought about it in the same way, I mean – that every experience of life, every input through the senses, is lodged in your unconscious. Of course it goes into the conscious mind first and then gradually sinks – it's so difficult not to use spatial imagery, you know, but there's really nothing spatial about it at all – into the unconscious: a sort of deposit or sediment. Now sometimes we make every effort to forget a memory: to sink it so far down in the unconscious that recovery becomes very difficult. That's because it's unpleasant. At other times a memory sinks of its own accord: it's just jostled out of the way by the pressure of daily living.'

'Yes, yes, I see,' said Wickfield. 'Is that where hypnosis comes in?'

'Inspector, you're hurrying me! Please don't hurry me. But yes, you're right. Freud thought there were only two ways to reach into the unconscious – two ways apart from active memory, that is, on which we depend daily for an awareness of our own selves and our continuity as individuals. Unless you're a Buddhist, of course, but that's a different matter! Where was I? Oh, yes, two ways to delve into the unconscious: dreams and hypnosis. What happens is this. Characteristic of both conditions – dreams and hypnosis, I mean - is the inactivity of the ego. It's the ego that blocks difficult or distant memories; so when it's inactive, the memories are free to float to the surface of the unconscious and be scooped up. An expert practitioner, like a hypnotherapist, can, if she is on hand, grab those memories as they float around.' She beamed on them, luxuriating in the confidence of her own prowess.

'Please tell us about Rachel.'

'Yes, well, Rachel explained her problem to me. What she wanted was to recover her experience of the snatch of conversation. At five years old she would be quite capable of absorbing an average adult conversation – not every word or turn of phrase, perhaps, but certainly the gist of it, and maybe a good deal more than that. She had it in her mind that the conversation she had overheard was revelatory, that is, that it contained the germs of information that would lead the police to her father's killer.'

'So what did you do?'

'Well, we tried hypnosis straight away, and I'm glad to say that it worked a treat. You see, we could have tried dreams first. Now, where dreams are concerned, I tend to go with Jung rather than Freud. Jung amended, or perhaps a better word would be extended, Freud - '

'That's very interesting, Mrs Braithwaite, but could you just tell us how you were able to help Rachel?'

'Yes, of course. You're quite right to rein me in, Inspector, otherwise I'd be all over the place! Now, Rachel. Well, Rachel was easily induced into a hypnotic state. When she was under, I questioned her about her experience as a five-year-old, and bit by bit we dredged this painful memory up from the depths. We had perhaps a dozen sessions in all. I would scribble down what she told me in her trance, and then we would go over it together to knock it into coherent shape.'

'So how reliable is it?'

'That's a good question, Inspector, and I'm not sure I've got a very positive answer. The trouble is, you see, that her memory as a five-year-old is inevitably coloured by her present experiences as an adult. Where she couldn't remember a word exactly, she would be tempted to make it up to convince herself that she was accurate in her memory. She would be so keen to succeed, that discretion would go out of the window. Because I wasn't on the inside of her memory, I had no means of gauging the accuracy of what was coming up in the hypnosis. On the other hand, as she gained in self-confidence, in trust in the hypnotic process, she was able to refine her first memories and weed out the accretions of her adult mind. Does that make sense?'

'Perfectly, thank you, Mrs Braithwaite. You have been admirably clear. You've obviously remembered these sheets. What is your abiding professional impression?'

'Well, Inspector, some of it is obviously too awkward to be true. I mean,' she said, as she reached for the papers again, 'no one would say "I'm off to France for a life-time": it's just not English. I'm not quite sure what she has misheard there, and it wouldn't be safe, or professional, for me to guess, but I had hopes that, in time, she would improve her version and make more sense of it. I'm so sorry I can't be of greater help. Really I'm no better at telling you what this conversation means than you are. You're on your own, Inspector!'

'Just one thing, though, Mrs Braithwaite: have you any explanation for the word "Baxter" at the end of the transcript?'

'Well, I have and I haven't.'

'Could you be a little more explicit?'

'You're in a great hurry, Inspector. I was about to explain when you interrupted me. She kept on coming up with the name Baxter. She remembered it had something to do with the conversation, but she didn't think it indicated the visitor's name. She was a bit puzzled by it and admitted that. So we just let it stand there, dangling, so to speak.'

The detectives thanked Mrs Braithwaite, Registered Hypnotherapist, for her time and her patience. They left her in no doubt that she had furthered their inquiry significantly. The willing shouldering of her responsibilities as a law-abiding citizen was commended.

*I*t being by then that time of evening, the two men slipped into the Bottle and Brush to discuss at length and in depth, over a pint of ale, the implications of their interview with the divine Mrs Braithwaite. The inspector's favourite tipple was tea, but he was happy on occasion to oblige Spooner by indulging in something stronger. They sat inconspicuously in a corner, underneath a wall-light and as far away from the muzak as possible, and began to tease apart the all-important conversation as recovered from Rachel's unconscious – or id, as it should, according to Mrs Braithwaite, be called.

'Where on earth do we start, Sir?' asked Spooner, taking a sip from his frothing glass.

'The first thing is that our Mick has gone,' said Wickfield. 'Instead we've apparently got a horse called Dream Chick. That's a bit of a change! OK, let's accept Mrs Braithwaite's caution that not everything recovered from Rachel's, er, id is going to be accurate. Let's also accept from Mrs Braithwaite that the consultations had not run their proper course and that Rachel's reconstructed memory was therefore still sketchy. The question is, can we accept the general drift of her notes as being a fair account of the conversation? We've no choice, really, because it's all we've got. So what do you think we can legitimately deduce?'

'Well, Sir,' said Spooner, clearing his throat portentously. 'There's a horse. It's roan, it's too frisky for Appleton's liking, it's a racing horse, and he's put in the highest bid he's prepared to make. His visitor, on the other hand, is confident he can do a deal and, what's more, that the horse is a winner.'

Here he consulted the papers once more.

'The visitor intends to live in France – if we can trust that bit – and all he needs is Len's cooperation to bring off the scoop of a lifetime. Unfortunately, as far as our visitor is concerned, Len lacks the spirit of adventure: he's an old stick-in-the-mud, he's looking a gift-horse in the mouth – whatever that means –

'It's not quite the phrase you're looking for, I fear.'

' – well, anyway, the visitor berates Len for failing to seize a golden opportunity. Len, for his part, accuses his visitor of being less than honest and of being a spendthrift.'

'If we're right, the visitor is so enraged with Leonard's attitude that he throttles him. What loss or failure did he fear if Leonard didn't go in with him in the purchase of the horse?'

'We don't really know, do we? All he says is that it's the chance he's been waiting for.'

'What do you make of the phrase, "She's a handsome roan, but the mount you want does not respond?" That doesn't seem to make much sense.'

'Perhaps she misheard. Perhaps the real words were, "If only I'd known – but count me out, Raymond - or Richmond or Desmond or Edmond or Drummond or Hammond or Esmond or even Rosamond".'

'No, no, not yet another name! I couldn't bear it; and in any case, you're forcing the rhythm. We'll leave that phrase out: it's probably not important, anyway. So we need to chase up a roan called Dream Chick which was put up for sale in 1951 for a large sum of money. That shouldn't be too difficult.'

Fifteen

A few words with Weatherbys produced the information that Dream Chick was sired by Forlorn (born such-and-such a date, of genetic strength such-and-such, career earnings such a sum of money) out of Plymouth Gumshoe (ditto) and was a three-year-old filly which ran in this race and that race. There was a huge amount of information, and Wickfield and Spooner also found themselves gazing at a photograph of the horse.

'One horse looks just like another to me, Sir,' Spooner confessed when they were alone. 'Bites you one end, wets you the other, and throws you into oblivion if you climb on its back – that is, if it hasn't trampled you into the field beforehand.'

'Spooner, don't be such a philistine. The horse is the king of animals, bred for beauty and strength, and where would society be without its racing fraternity? Think of all the employment provided by studs, stables, race-courses, betting-shops, animal foodstuff manufacturers, farriery, veterinary surgery, hunting outfitters – and so on and so forth. The list is just too long. No, no, we're entering a noble and entrancing world here.'

'Except we're not entering it, are we, Sir? All we need to know is who proposed to Leonard Appleton to buy a horse called – I ask you! – Dream Chick.'

'You're right, of course. I was getting carried away. Not that I've been to a race-meeting or hunt in my life: I was just being frivolous.'

Their research was swifter and easier than they had feared. Thanks to the activities of the Jockey Club and the British

Horseracing Authority, through the family firm of Weatherbys they were able to establish that the last owner of Dream Chick was a countrywoman called Helen Venn-Rivière, who lived in a stately pile just west of Hereford (as it transpired). The fine summer weather was an admirable accompaniment to their thirty-mile drive. The A4103 was not conducive to speed, but neither of them felt that their arrival at Lanrym Hall was so urgent that they needed to exercise undue haste; they were content to motor down tranquilly, enjoying the unmatched glories of an English shire. It was mid-morning when they drove sedately through the ample gates of the house and up a long, straight drive lined for the most part with centennial beeches. A rise in the ground prevented sight of the house until the visitors were less than two hundred yards away. The Queen Anne mansion, in dark brown brick, square, solid and yet elegant, stood three storeys high, with dormer windows in the roof to illuminate the servants' rooms. (Those were the days, thought Wickfield.) Tall chimneys rose on either side of the house, giving it a sense of lightness and grace. The oblong sash window-frames and the front-door were painted white. The round lawn in front of the house was host to an immense cedar of Lebanon, while behind the house, in a thick band of brilliant greens, mixed groups of native trees sheltered the house from the north wind.

The two men had only just alighted when their hostess, or the châtelaine as they immediately thought of her, emerged at the top of the short flight of steps that led to the front-door. Of average height and build, she yet impressed with an air of poise and authority. Her reddish-gingery hair was perched on top of her head like the crest of a pineapple, while a round, pretty face smiled beguilingly beneath. She was wearing a loose jumper, baggy trousers and suede bootees. Altogether she made a handsome picture. For a woman of fifty she had worn well.

'Helen Venn-Rivière,' she announced, as she descended the steps with her right hand extended in welcome. The men were not slow to approach, and the three walked round the house to a small topiaried garden where a table had been laid for refreshments. Wickfield outlined the subject of their inquiry.

'I'm intrigued to know why a horse that's been dead for nearly twenty years should be of interest to you, Gentlemen,' she said. 'She wasn't murdered, you know: we had to have her put down after an accident. Or perhaps you call that murder?'

'No, no, Mrs Venn-Rivière –

'Please call me Helen: that's what everybody does round here.'

'Very well – Helen. It's nothing like that. I don't think we're free just yet to divulge all the ins and outs of the case, but it boils down to this. Twenty years ago, two men fell out over this horse. We know who one of them was; we are anxious to discover the identity of the other.'

'And how can I help?'

'Did you put the horse up for sale in the spring of 1951?'

'Now let me see. The spring of 1951? Yes, we did, briefly, but she didn't sell. At least, we were not willing to part with her for any sum that interested parties offered. You see, she was a very promising horse, with plenty of prize-money behind her and excellent prospects.'

'May I ask how much you were asking? The question is relevant, I assure you.'

'Without checking in my books, I should say round the 200 guinea mark.'

'And what money might she have earnt if she had lived?'

'Oh, twenty times that much, I should think.'

'Now do you remember any particular potential purchaser who tried to haggle with you? He might have said something about having to satisfy a partner.'

'Well, now, let me see. There was that odious little man from over Brecon way: what was his name? No, I can't remember. Then there was that quite ghastly woman from the Normanby stables. No, no, it wasn't her. Oh, yes, I know who you might mean: Templar Buxton. How could I forget a name like that! Big chap, bit aggressive, I thought. Yes, he did his best to get the horse, but he just didn't have the money. Tried to knock us down; tried very hard, in fact, but we weren't desperate to sell, so his efforts came to nothing.'

'And did he mention any partner?'

'Yes, he did, but I can't recall the name. Not a local, I seem to remember. Mr Buxton mentioned him because he thought that his name might carry some weight with me: a sort of respectable guarantee.'

'Right, Helen, what can you tell us about this Mr Buxton?'

'Not much. He drove over one day in some sort of land-rover-type vehicle, one that had seen better days. He swaggered in, asked to see the horse, asked some questions about her and offered us 100 guineas. Seemed very keen but got quite annoyed when we wouldn't accept his offer: ridiculously low it was, as you can appreciate. She was a valuable horse.'

'Can you remember where he came from?'

'No, reasonably local, I think. Somewhere between here and Leominster? But he's not going to be of much help to you since he's dead.'

'Dead?' said Wickfield. 'Ah, that certainly puts a different complexion on matters. When was this?'

'Not long after, actually. He shot himself, apparently. Something to do with his wife or girl-friend, I think. Or was it financial ruin staring him in the face? Or the diagnosis of an incurable disease? No, it's gone. Sorry; but I know where I read it: the local paper. The forename Templar leapt out at me from the page.'

'Would you have any record of his address?'

'No, no, because no business was ever concluded between us.'

'Might he have left a card in case you changed your mind?'

'He might have, Inspector, but why should I keep it all these years?'

'Might your husband know where he lived?'

'No, he wouldn't. I deal with all the buying and selling of the bloodstock. I think I can justifiably boast that I have a better eye for a good animal than he does, and he's happy to leave it all to me.'

'Well, you've been very helpful,' said Wickfield. 'Thank you so much for your time.'

After a little more desultory conversation, the two rose and left.

Wickfield thought that on the whole they had not done badly. An unusual name was a start in a new phase of the inquiry.

'Well, Spooner, any thoughts?' he asked, as they drove slowly down the drive. The sergeant said nothing for a moment as he moved over to share the tarmac with an incoming vehicle and then to negotiate the gates on to the road.

'Well, Sir, the information is all very sketchy, isn't it? Thin, very thin. But what about this? Templar Buxton kills Appleton because his

155

hopes of a fortune are dashed; a dream collapses. Then he takes his own life because he can't face the future. Then his wife, or perhaps a son, or a cousin, takes revenge on Appleton's daughter: an eye for an eye, and all that caper.'

'It's a start, I'll give you that. A shaky one, but definitely a hypothesis. Let's try and put it to the test. But I wish people would realise that revenge is God's business, not ours. That would save us a lot of trouble.'

It took little trouble to trace the late Templar Buxton's widow to a small house in Worcester: small and, if the truth be told, rather mean. Mrs Buxton presented a drab appearance: perhaps she felt that life had not been kind to her and that her dress should reflect her disappointment for all the world to see. When Wickfield and Spooner called on her that afternoon, she was hanging washing out in the back garden and asked her callers whether they would mind waiting until she had finished. Mrs Buxton was stout and unkempt, but her voice and speech betrayed a good education and a more gracious past than the present would suggest. She had simply let herself go. She was very surprised by the policemen's visit. She brought them into the house rather than leave them on the doorstep – the front-door opened directly into a small sitting-room – but forgot to ask them to be seated while she disappeared out the back to conclude her laundry.

'I can't think what you want with me, Gentlemen,' she said as she returned, wiping her hands on her dirty apron. 'Since my husband's death, and particularly since my son left home, I've taken less and less interest in what goes on around me and, to coin a phrase, I don't know nuffink about nuffink. Sorry. You'll probably feel you've come to quite the wrong house.' This was uttered in a flat tone that suggested that she did not really care one way or the other.

'You are Mrs Emily Buxton, widow of Templar Buxton?'

'Yes, what of it?'

'May we sit down a moment, Mrs Buxton, but we shan't keep you a few minutes?'

'Yes, go ahead.'

Various items were removed from the chairs so that the guests could take advantage of Mrs Buxton's permission to be seated.

'Did your husband ever know a man called Leonard Appleton, a Worcester businessman?'

'Yes, he did. He mentioned him from time to time.'

'How did they meet, do you know?'

'Yes, it was at a race-meeting. They got talking, and Len invited Templar to join him at another meeting later on.'

'Did they always meet at race-courses, never at home?'

'Oh, I wouldn't know about that, but Len never came to my house once Templar and I had got married, I do know that.'

'How well do you think they knew each other?'

'Well, Templar said Len was a good sort, generous with his cash at a meeting, but apart from the interest in racing, I'm not sure they had a great deal in common.'

'How long did they know each other, Mrs Buxton?'

'How long? Oh, ten years, maybe.'

'Do you know that your husband once approached Len Appleton about buying a race-horse together?'

'No, that's news to me. How do you know?'

'It's information from the then owner of the horse. Tell me, were they still in touch when your husband died?'

'No, there was a row of some sort, don't know what.'

'Can you remember when?'

'No, not really, perhaps a year before Templar died.'

'Do you know of anybody else in whom your husband might have confided about buying a race-horse?'

'No. No, I don't. I had no interest in racing, and Templar wouldn't have bothered to tell me anything: he'd know it would bore me silly.'

'Could you bear to tell us about your husband's death, Mrs Buxton?'

'Oh, yes, it's a long time ago now, but I can't think what you want to know for. There was nothing suspicious about it.'

'Please go on.'

'Despite his blustering and his bullying ways, Templar was at heart a sensitive man. He lacked confidence and made up for it by trying to impress everyone with his masculinity and authority. Petty, really, but then he wasn't the only one. Anyway, he began to feel that he was a failure. Nothing seemed to go right for him. I tried to get him to share his troubles, but he was too diffident, or ashamed, or perhaps confused. He got into debt, and one day he blew his brains out. That's about the size of it.'

'Was there an inquest?'

'Of course.'

'And what was the verdict, if I may ask?'

'Suicide while the balance of his mind was disturbed – the usual catch-all phrase.'

'How did you manage after that?'

'Not very well, I'm afraid. I was no good without Templar. Our son was only eight, and I had to keep going for his sake, but I lost interest, really. I sold the house to pay our debts and moved into this little terrace, where I've been ever since. Since Nat went, I sometimes wonder why I keep going, that's the honest truth.'

'Tell us about Nat, Mrs Buxton.'

'Between you and me, he's a bit of a disappointment, but I blame myself, you see. I couldn't do much with him: I was all to pieces myself. He got into a bad crowd at school, even though academically he did all right, and he started smoking and drinking even before he was a teenager. I kept reminding him of his big house and his prep school before his father died, of the hopes his father had nourished in his regard, of what he could make of himself if he only put his mind to it. Of course, I was no example, I know that. He'd only to look at me to see that I didn't practise what I preached. Not much of a mother, I'm sorry to say. However, he did get a decent girl-friend once who tried to make something of him, but it didn't last. Hey, now I come to think of it, her name was Appleton – or if it wasn't, it was something very like: Appleyard, Appleby, Appleford?'

'Where is he now, Mrs Buxton? I think it might help us to have a word with him if his girl-friend really was an Appleton.'

'Don't know what for. What's he got to do with all this? Just because he knew a girl called Appleton – if it was Appleton.'

'Perhaps nothing, but we should like to check for ourselves.'

'What's all this about, anyway?' the widow asked. 'Why all this interest?'

'Just routine inquiries, Mrs Buxton,' Spooner reassured her soothingly. 'It'll probably all come to nothing.'

'Oh, well, have it your own way. Don't bother to come again, Gentlemen: I don't know anything else.'

'Where can we get in touch with Nat, please?' Wickfield asked, and when they had a home address and a works address, the policemen left the widow to her wonderings – or probably her lack of wonderings.

From being a spotty, spindly youth of twenty-one, Nathaniel Buxton had matured into a spotty, spindly youth of twenty-five. His father's death and his mother's subsequent personal, financial and social decline had embittered him. It is useless to inquire what sort of a man he would have turned out to be if fate had been kinder to him. There is no reason to think that he would have turned out any worse than most children of the Sixties. Children's characters are supposedly formed by the age of five - and well before that according to some - and Nat's woes did not begin until three years after that. The problem was that his opportunities for self-improvement, for travel, for the broadening of his horizons, for the cultivation of the finer human sentiments were limited by his mother's loss of zest. At school – the Westfield Grammar School in the city – he had done reasonably well, without thereby endearing himself to his peers, and after school, instead of attempting further education, he applied to enter the fire service and was accepted: his height was adequate, he did not need spectacles, he was eighteen, in good health and able to pass the literacy and numeracy tests to which he allowed himself to submit. His application to join the fire service was dictated not by the pedestrian desire merely to earn a living but by a genuine wish to benefit his fellow humans in a direct and active way. After a year or two, he was transferred to the Evesham Fire Service in Merstow Street, and it was during his employment there that he and Rachel Appleton made their acquaintance. They were standing side by side in a cinema queue when some hitch delayed the opening of the doors: perhaps it was a power cut, or the sticking of a fire exit. They got chatting, and in a little time they had watched the film together, shared a bag of popcorn, exchanged phone numbers and arranged to meet again.

On one of their outings, Rachel had confided to her beloved the thoughts of revenge nurtured in her bosom since the age of five, and he seemed to understand. Whether he had thoughts of revenge of his own Inspector Wickfield was determined to discover.

He and Spooner sent word forward that they would like to have a short conversation with Nathaniel Buxton, if that were possible without disrupting the workings of the fire service, and when they turned up at Merstow Street, young Buxton was waiting for them, in some perplexity, be it said, being unaware of having fallen foul of the law in any capacity. Wickfield had the merest adumbration of a suspicion, suggested without depth of fact by his sergeant, and he was not going to blunder into a conversation with accusations and wild speculations that might antagonise the partner of their conversation. On the other hand, it would be very interesting if Nat Buxton and Rachel Appleton had been acquainted. Wickfield made it his business to put Buxton at his ease and to be amicable. The interview took place in one of the offices in the fire-station.

'Mr Buxton, let me say at the outset that we are carrying out routine investigations into the death of Rachel Carver at the beginning of the year and that therefore you are concerned only because your father and her father are known to have had a row. You see, we are taking the line that Rachel's death is connected with that of her father in 1951, although we haven't yet been able to establish a direct link.'

Nat Buxton viewed the two men, not with antipathy, for which he had no cause, but with indifference. His less than attractive exterior need not reflect a less than attractive interior, Wickfield reminded himself, as he often had to. Wickfield imagined that behind those incurious eyes lay a warm and sagacious personality brimming over with the milk of human kindness.

'Inspector, I know nothing of any row between my father and Rachel Carver's father. Why on earth should I?'

'Ah, sorry, I forgot to tell you that Rachel's father was Leonard Appleton of Worcester.'

Buxton absorbed this piece of intelligence. It seemed to take a little effort to digest.

'I see,' he said. 'Yes, I knew Leonard Appleton by name. I also knew his daughter.'

'Yes, your mother gave us to understand that. Perhaps you'd care to tell us about it, Sir.'

'There's really nothing to tell. Rachel and I met in the September of 1967, when she was twenty-one and I was twenty-four. We dated for about six months and then, by mutual consent, parted. That's about all there is to it.'

'Did you meet her family?'

'If by family you mean her aunt and her aunt's children, yes, I did.'

'Did they ever talk about Leonard's death?'

'Occasionally, yes.'

'Did you know that Rachel overheard some of the conversation that her father held with his attacker?'

'Yes, I knew that: she told me.'

'What else did she tell you?'

'That all she really remembered was her father addressing the man as Mick, but that she was positive that she would recognise the visitor's voice again.'

'Did she ever talk to you about getting her revenge?'

'Yes, that rather spooked me, I'm afraid. You see, it was an obsession with her, and she spent all her available time listening out in public places for this man's voice. All a bit weird, I thought.'

'May I ask why you separated?'

'No reason. Neither of us thought the relationship was going anywhere in particular, and we agreed to call it a day. It was perfectly amicable. Nothing sinister, if that's what you're getting at.'

'No, no, we never imagined there was. Can we move on to some slightly more awkward matters? What do you remember of your own father's death?'

'What has my father's death got to do with my going out with Rachel? It's not at all clear to me what you're getting at, Inspector. Sorry.'

'That will become clearer in a minute, I hope, Mr Buxton. Just tell us what you remember of your father's death, in particular the reasons why your father might have wished to take his own life.'

'I know only what my mother told me. My father had problems, she said, probably financial, I don't know. She also told me, which I had never realised, that my father was insecure and had very low self-esteem. You could have fooled me. Anyway, his death seems to have been due to a combination of things.'

'Did your mother ever blame Mr Appleton in any way?'

'No, why on earth should she?'

'Well, as I said, Appleton and your father had a row not long before your father's death. A suspicious mind might make a connexion.'

'I'm not quite with you, Inspector. You'll have to enlighten me.'

'OK, let's just speculate; but please be assured that we are not making accusations – not at this stage. Your father went to Len Appleton one evening to persuade him to join him in buying a promising race-horse, a three-year-old roan filly – '

'How do you know that? My mother never said anything about that to me.'

'No, she didn't know – at least, we don't think she did. The fact is that a few months before Rachel met her death, she went to a hypnotherapist in an effort to recover her memories of that last conversation of her father's. That was one of the things that came out of her sessions. Mr Appleton apparently – we're still going by Rachel's memories - refused point blank to go in with your father's scheme, and the conversation ended in a fatal struggle. If Rachel told you that she overheard some of it, you probably know that the two men started shouting at each other, and then the mysterious visitor strangled Mr Appleton, we presume in anger rather than in a calculated or premeditated manner – not that that makes any difference, really. His murderer has never been identified, but we were wondering whether it could have been your father.'

'My father's name wasn't Mick, or anything like it. Rachel was quite clear that her father's aggressor was called Mick, so it can't have been my father.'

'Well, that's the point, Sir. We think she misheard Dream Chick, which was the name of the horse your father wanted to buy but didn't have the cash for. So the name Mick is a complete red herring.'

'This is nonsense, Inspector. I can't entertain it for a moment. My father blustered and bullied, but he wasn't violent.'

'Well, we further speculated – please forgive me, Mr Buxton – that your father committed suicide either because his financial affairs were in disarray or because he felt guilty about Len Appleton's death, or perhaps out of a combination of both reasons. Then a member of his family, perhaps you yourself, took revenge on Appleton's daughter. You see, the motive was there: your father died because Len Appleton refused to help him, and now a member of the family has got his or her own back.'

'Inspector, I must protest: you haven't a shred of evidence. These are the wildest accusations I've ever heard.'

'I'm very glad to hear that, Mr Buxton, but perhaps you wouldn't mind just telling us where you were on the night Rachel was murdered.'

'I'm not sure I wish to cooperate any further, Inspector. I think you have a damned nerve, if you don't mind my saying so.'

'Mr Buxton, it's in your own interests just as much as in ours that you can be eliminated from the picture. Believe me, we don't wish to involve you any more than we need.'

'What date are we talking about?'

'12 January.'

'How do I know? It's anybody's guess.'

'Well, we won't press you now, but we'd like a statement from you, very soon, preferably by tonight, about your movements on that day between four o'clock and six o'clock. Please be as detailed as possible. Makes it easier for us.'

Nat Buxton's alibi was solid. He had checked the fire service roster, and he had been on duty from one in the afternoon till nine o'clock at night. That meant that he was in the fire-station all that time, except for two calls they had: one was to a crash on the A38, one was to a small fire in a builder's yard. The records of his presence were available for all to see, if the inspector liked to go along and check for himself. The names of his colleagues were listed, and the name of the officer in charge. There would doubtless be wages' lists available for inspection. He was deeply satisfied that the records supported his story, and he hoped the policemen would withdraw their unworthy suspicions and refrain from hassling him in the future.

'That sort of vituperation is all we get for being polite and patient, Spooner, my lad. It saps one's faith in human nature. Not that my faith has ever been very strong, but you know what I mean.'

Leaving nothing to chance, Wickfield instructed Spooner to repair post haste to Evesham – the following morning – and to check with the fire-station. Buxton's alibi was unassailable. Hell's teeth.

Sixteen

*T*his was undoubtedly a disappointment. Wickfield, and Spooner with him, had been growing increasingly confident that an arrest was in the offing, with only some cogent evidence to marshal. Wickfield suggested they slept on it. It is just not possible, he opined, that the murderer was someone of whose existence they were as yet unaware. The original inquiry had spread the net far and wide; their own researches had drawn in new strands. There was simply no new personage who could enter the scene, unless one were going to resort to the intervention of a supernatural or paranormal power. This meant that one of the persons already known to be connected with either Leonard Appleton or his daughter must be the murderer of one or of both victims. Wickfield proposed that they independently went over the *dramatis personae* yet again, and they would reconvene in the morning to thrash the matter out over a pot of tea. All the materials of the case were there – like discarded tea-leaves; they were just not being read aright.

On the following morning, therefore, the two convened in the inspector's exiguous office for a summit meeting. The details of the investigation were before them: witness and interview statements, tables of dates and timings, maps, street-plans, the various hypotheses they had already advanced, the files of the original inquiry. Wickfield flourished new sheets of paper on which to record their present thoughts. Tea and biscuits were produced. Wickfield asked the desk not to put through any phone-calls for the time being and to inform all and sundry that no disturbance would be countenanced. Let the conference commence!

'You know, Spooner,' Wickfield began, 'I think we can put not the slightest reliance on anything Rachel Carver ever said. We've had her thoughts transmitted to us by her aunt Sarah, her husband Andy, her boyfriend Nat and the hypnotherapist Mrs Braithwaite, and I think we can discount them all.'

'Why is that, Sir?'

'Well, take the hypnotherapist first. Nice woman. Honest, caring. She was fully aware that Rachel's notes were inchoate, and she warned us about taking them too seriously. Now none of the Buxton-Appleton saga, as it has come down to us through her, is corroborated by anyone involved. Mrs Buxton and her son Nat disclaim all knowledge of it. Mrs Venn-Rivière cannot remember the name of Buxton's partner. The horse existed all right, and Buxton may have put in a bid for it, but we have no confirmation whatever that Appleton was involved.'

'So what do you think happened, Sir?'

'I think this. Unfortunately it's guess-work, and we're never going to be able to prove it, but here goes. Rachel is taken to a race-meeting by her father, when she is, say, four or five years old. They are met by Templar Buxton, who has made a habit of attending meetings with Appleton. In the course of conversation, Buxton tells Appleton, in passing, that he has been trying to buy a filly called Dream Chick but has not succeeded. Perhaps Buxton does ask Appleton to go in with him, the same as he may have asked other acquaintances interested in horse-racing. Perhaps they even had words over it, but Len says no. They then go on to discuss the price of garden peas or the state of the weather in Matabeleland. Rachel, however, has latched on to the horse's name: Dream Chick. For a five-year-old, it smacks of fairy-tale or whatever else has caught her imagination in her short life. When she later, twenty years later, comes to recall a snatch of the conversation in which her father is killed, her memory is overlaid, or obstructed, or twisted, by the recurrent and insistent name of this horse. Her hypnosis notes distort everything in terms of a blooming filly!

'As for the information passed on to us by Mrs Aunt Platt, she admits that at the time of Len Appleton's death the poor girl was traumatised. Why do we think that Rachel's memory of the event is going to be any clearer when she tells Nat and Andy about it years later? She's got a bee in her bonnet about somebody called Mick, and nothing will shift it. Perhaps she did overhear something of the conversation; perhaps one of the words was Mick or something like it; but we're never going to find out. In my view, therefore, Nat Buxton and his entire family can be eliminated forthwith from the inquiry. A complete red herring. What do you say?'

'But Edwin Jones gave independent corroboration of some of the conversation, Sir. Is that not valid either?'

'Well, what did Jones actually tell us? It amounts to virtually nothing. He admitted first of all that he could hear anything at all only when the voices were raised in anger. He then comes up with two – just two – pieces of information: the word Mick and the word bankrupt. But the thing is, he's not really sure of either. He can't be, really. He was probably half-seas-over, anyway.'

'Hm, yes, Sir. That's all very disappointing. We've wasted quite a bit of time there.'

'OK, so much for me. Have you come up with anything a little more cheerful, Sergeant?'

'Well, Sir, rather than start with the *dramatis personae*, as you suggested, I started at the other end, with the crimes.'

Wickfield raised a disbelieving eyebrow. 'Is that so?' he eventually managed, facetiously.

'Yes, Sir, might give us a new perspective, I thought. Sir.'

'Spooner, don't be so bashful! Since when have I objected to initiative? You are absolutely right to begin where you like, and more power to you. Now deliver!'

'Well, Sir, let's leave aside for the moment whether the crimes are connected. Take Len Appleton's death, first. The murderer must be a man. We have two reasons for this. Both Rachel and Edwin heard a man's voice, and I presume that we are not going to discount that piece of evidence? And a woman would not have been capable of overpowering Len in a fight and strangling him to death. At least, I don't think she would. Now the motive for that crime. Nothing in the house was disturbed, except for the broken furniture in the sitting-room, and entry wasn't forced – that is, if Appleton had already locked his doors - so we can rule out burglary. Furthermore, Edwin's testimony stands – possibly – to the extent of limiting the murderer to Appleton's friends, to someone with whom he has made an appointment and with whom he can converse in his sitting-room.

That leaves a personal motive. We have found no evidence of a rival in love or in business. Our difficulty there is that the original inquiry ransacked the range of Appleton's friends and came out negative. But then to opportunity. Anyone could have been the mysterious visitor, without necessarily being able to produce a viable alibi. Not to have an alibi is not a crime. On the other hand, we know Edwin Jones was on the spot. It's a pity the trial acquitted him: he could have been very useful to us, but unless we come up with some compelling new evidence, he's a lost cause.'

'So have you a tentative conclusion at this stage, Sergeant?'

'Well, we seem to be left to choose among the Napiers, Noel, Michael and Victor. You have said we should discount Templar Buxton. So that's not a long list, is it? And several other people we've come across I shouldn't necessarily trust very far, but they were either too young – Andy Carver – or, as far as we can tell, not on the scene at the time -- Peabody.'

'Good, Spooner, good. I like this a lot. You've done all my work for me!'

'Thank you, Sir. Now on to Rachel's murder. Because of where the body was put, we think it was a local man. I say "man", mostly because no woman is in the frame, but I suppose a woman would have been physically capable of moving the body. It has to be someone who owns, or has access to, a Browning pistol. That could be almost anybody. As far as opportunity is concerned, all our chief suspects could have been around at the time: all three Napiers were in the country, so was Edwin – sorry, I forgot we can't include him - so was Peabody, so was Andy. The motive, we decided long ago, was personal, and the discovery of the handbag, with a cheque-book and a purse still inside, confirmed this diagnosis.'

'"Diagnosis", Sergeant? We're not running a clinic, you know.'

'No, Sir.' He decided to disregard the interruption and continue. 'So what motives are we left with? We can discount rape and sexual assault, as the *post mortem* revealed nothing in that line. That would certainly let Andy out. All the other five male suspects are thirty years or so older than Rachel: does that suggest that they may have a connexion with Len's death?

'The alibis are not impressive. Let's just run over them again. The crucial time is between four fifteen, when Rachel left home to plant evidence on Michael Napier, and five forty-five, when she was due to show up at a greasy spoon to celebrate with Andy. An hour and a half on a January afternoon. Days slowly lengthening, but still getting dark by four. Now where were our men between those times? Noel Napier, the eldest brother, claims to have been at work until getting home at about half-past five. From the city he would need to allow twenty minutes anyway to get home. From half-past five onwards, he was at home with Shirley and his brother Victor, chatting, having supper, playing cards, but that takes us way beyond the time of Rachel's murder. On to Michael. He was at work until half-past five, when he walked directly to the pub to meet his old chum Justin Blackwater. He was in the pub for an hour. That all seems above board. And so to the third brother. Victor's alibi overlaps with Noel's, but the first part of our window is not accounted for. He can't account for his whereabouts until a quarter past five, when his sister-in-law came home. Yes, weak, distinctly weak. Another weak alibi is that furnished by our ex-army friend Grimwold Peabody, who says he was at home for the whole time in question. The only saving grace is that he claims to have made a phone-call to his sister at five p.m., and that, if true, would probably rule him out, because physically he couldn't have covered all the movements we know the murderer took. Finally, if we included our cabinetmaking friend Edwin, he says he might have been at work. His wife tells us that he came home shortly before six. He's our prime suspect, if you ask me – for both murders. But no, the British legal system has said No, so that's that. I'll say no more. May I make a suggestion, Sir?'

'Of course, go ahead.'

'A couple of phone-calls would probably clear up some of the alibis. Should we reconvene when we've made them?'

'You're right, of course. This conference verges on the hasty and unprepared. My apologies. Can I leave the donkey-work to you while I try to sort out next month's conference in Blackpool, and we'll meet again in an hour, say?'

The resumed conference took place, after an extension requested by the sergeant, in a sombre atmosphere. Was the case going to remain unsolved for lack of hard evidence? The heavens forfend. Time, however, was running out; so were their options.

'So, Spooner, what have you got for us?'

'Some good news and some bad news, Sir.'

'Right, I'll have the good news first.'

'The good news is that I have been successful in chasing up alibis. Noel had a conference with a client that lasted from quarter-past four until after five, when he left for home. He simply couldn't have got to Evesham in time to do any damage. We know Michael Napier was at work and then walked to the pub. Victor's neighbour, or rather Noel and Shirley's neighbour, a Mrs Slattery, who lived on the opposite side of their house to the church, has a distinct memory of that afternoon, because she was expecting the delivery of a new fridge, stayed at home and kept looking out of the window. Several times she went to the front gate to look down the road, and she remembers seeing Victor on several occasions, either in the garden practising his golf-swings, or in the house, where lights went on and off as he moved about. So he was definitely at home for the whole time we're interested in. And finally Peabody. I checked up on that phone-call to his sister, and it went through at exactly 5.01 and lasted three minutes.'

'So don't tell me the bad news: let me guess. We haven't got any suspects left!'

'Exactly, Sir. Depressing, or what?'

'We're not beaten, Sergeant, far from it. I'm going to put my thinking cap on, and I shall come back to you with a solution, mark my words.'

'Yes, Sir,' said Spooner dutifully, the words oozing incredulity.

It was late when Wickfield got home, and supper was ready. His domestic routine, in so far as it could be maintained, was very precious to him, because it centred round colloquies with his wife of thirty years, Beth, an easy-going, comfortable sort of person with an interest in his work and the knack of stoking up the fires of his inner contentment. They had supper and then sat in the sitting-room with a pot of tea, continuing their supper chat prior to taking up a book each.

'I forgot to tell you last night of a really clever clue in yesterday's crossword,' Wickfield said conversationally.

'And what was that, dear?'

'The clue was, "Spot on patient's bottom beginning to congeal, cut from behind".'

'How many letters?'

'Five.'

'Had you got any?'

'I'm not telling you.'

Beth thought for a while. 'Nope,' she said, 'the answer eludes me. What was it?'

'Exact.'

'Clever, yes, very clever.' Beth spent a few seconds contemplating this neat and witty clue. 'Now let me tell you a joke – if you can call it a joke – which one of the doctors told us today. A man quoted the philosopher as saying, "I am, therefore I think". This is known as putting Descartes before the horse.'

'I think I've heard it before. It has a slight humour, I suppose,' her husband said grudgingly.

'I've been asking myself where the humour lies,' Beth ran on. 'It's obviously not in the first line, where the man gets the quotation back to front. It's in the incorporation of the philosopher's name into a common English expression, but if you explain it like that, it loses all its wit.'

'"The man gets it back to front". I think you've just solved my case for me. Many thanks, my dear Beth – and not for the first time.' Wickfield sat back with a huge grin on his face, while Beth looked on. She made no further comment but once again wondered at her husband's capacity for silly faces.

Excitedly the following morning, Wickfield asked Spooner to confirm that there was only client parking in front of the Barford Buildings in Evesham.

'Yes, I think that's correct, Sir, because the building is virtually on the pavement. There are a few spaces for clients at the front, but most of the parking, for most clients and for all staff, is at the back. What difference does it make?'

'It makes the difference between success and failure, Sergeant. Let's get going.'

They drove to Evesham, parked, with permission, at the back of Barford Buildings, and prepared their reconstruction.

'This is where you start your timings, Sergeant.'

From the back of the office-block, they walked into the High Street and down it, left into Oat Street, right into Cowl Street, and then, once over the river, they took in turn Port Street, Broadway Road, Davies Road, Falkland Road, Hazel Avenue, Poplar Close. In front of No.5 Poplar Close, they marked on their sheets a putative delay of five minutes before retracing their steps. They then got into their car, drove to Poplar Avenue, marked up another five minutes, drove to the Baptist chapel, recorded a delay of three minutes, returned to Poplar Close - a further delay of ten minutes - and finally returned to park at the back of Barford Buildings.

'Right, Sir,' Spooner said when he had drawn up the table of their route and timings, 'how do we explain to a jury what we've just been doing? What's in your mind?'

'This is what I think happened. Michael Napier is looking out of his office window one day when he sees passing by the girl who set him up for the jewellery robbery. He leaves by the back of the building and follows her.'

'Why the back, Sir? It would have been quicker by the front, surely?'

'Yes, probably, but he would certainly have been seen by the receptionist who is on duty downstairs all day long. As it was, if he was challenged – very unlikely – or questioned afterwards, he could always pretend he was getting a coffee, visiting another office or fetching something from his car. So, to continue. He follows Rachel, and is able to check, despite the gathering dusk, that it is the girl he remembers from a previous encounter that had promised to be erotic but was in fact a betrayal. Lo and behold, she makes for his house. There he watches aghast as she produces a key and enters without a backward glance. He follows her in, accosts her, shoots her, bundles her body into a black plastic bag or similar. He then walks casually but purposefully back to Barford Buildings, gets in his car, drives home, picks up the body, drives to the Baptist chapel and disposes of his burden. He then drives back to Barford Buildings, parks, and leaves on foot as usual for his rendez-vous with Justin Whatever-His-Name-Is.

'Now we know from Andy Carver that Rachel left the house at a quarter past four. She would therefore be walking past Napier's window at twenty past four. Our timings show that he could have started his chase at 4.20, committed the murder, disposed of the body

171

and be ready to meet his friend at the Golden Wheatsheaf at 5.35 - in seventy-five minutes. We allowed ten minutes on his return journey to check for traces of the dastardly deed in the house and in the boot of his car. When he returns to his office-block, he parks, enters by the back door and leaves by the front, making sure he is seen as usual by the receptionist, who is shortly going off duty. Remember, for most of this time daylight has vanished. He runs a risk, but one calculated to free him for ever from his past.'

'And what made you suddenly engineer this reconstruction, Sir?'

'It was my wife, really. Last night she told a bit of a joke in which a man mistook the front for the back of a phrase. That reminded me of the parking at Barford Buildings. I had been presuming all this time, at the back of my mind, that Napier's alibi was valid: he was at work in his office until he left at a little after half-past five. If he left the building at all to follow the girl or later to get to his car – and he would have needed his car to transport the body - he would be seen in reception. What, however, if he left the building by the back? His alibi was then torpedoed. The question was whether he could accomplish in the time available all we know happened over Rachel's death, and we have proved it could.'

'We have proved it could, Sir, but have we proved it did?'

'Well, there will be negative evidence that no one saw him in the office building during the time in question, that is, if people can remember that far back. Alternatively, someone may recall seeing him leaving the offices or walking down the High Street. Forensics will pick up something in his house or car, I daresay. We may be able to trace the purchase – or at least acquisition – of the gun to him. I owe you an apology: I blundered in accepting Napier's alibi at its face value, without thorough investigation. I'm sorry. It would have saved us a huge amount of trouble. Of course, if Napier is guilty of Rachel's murder, he was also guilty of Appleton's: he had no conceivable motive except to cover his tracks or prevent a disastrous disclosure. The first thing, though, I think, is to arrest him and see what transpires.'

The two men climbed slowly out of the car, made for the front of the building, approached the receptionist and inquired whether they could see Mr Napier on an important matter.

'Yes, by all means go up, Gentlemen. You know where his office is.'

As they reached the top of the third flight of steps and made for Napier's office, the object of their quest came out and came towards them.

'Gentlemen, I'm glad to see you. I've phoned my wife, and I'm ready to accompany you to the station to make a statement. I shan't be giving you any trouble. If you hadn't come to me, I'd have gone to you.'

'How did you know we were in the building, Sir?'

'The receptionist mentioned earlier that you had called again, and I took the opportunity to straighten a few affairs. She phoned me a few minutes ago to warn me that you were on your way up.'

Once in Worcester, with preliminaries worked through, Michael Napier sat down quite collectedly in one of the interview rooms to compose his confession.

I, Michael Napier, of 5 Poplar Close, Evesham, wish, of my own free will, to make the following statement, clarifying the events surrounding the deaths of Leonard Appleton and his daughter Rachel Carver. I do so, persuaded by my beloved wife Trudy that it is the best, and the only honourable, course of action. If she had acted unilaterally, as it were, and gone to the police before I was ready to accept full responsibility for my actions, what might that have done to our marriage? I was born in the same year as Len, 1916, and we attended the same school, where we were friendly but not friends. I saw him only rarely thereafter, but when, at the age of thirty-five, I had money troubles and had exhausted other avenues of assistance, I thought he might be sympathetic. I went to see him one evening, but, quite rightly, he refused to help. He had no reason to help, he said he could not afford it, and in any case, as I now recognise, for him it was too great a risk. I simply lost my temper; I was blind to reason. I punched him hard in the face, expecting to floor him and walk out, but he retaliated, and we fought. I saw red and strangled him. I was frightened and appalled at what I had done. Grabbing my coat, I fled into the night. The police came to interview me, along, seemingly, with half of Worcester, and I concocted a simple alibi which convinced them. The police told me I was a prime suspect because the girl had remembered the name Mick. What she actually heard was Hick, a private form of address between me and Len that goes back to our school-days. He was poking fun at my obsession with the folk-singer Hick Winters. No one else was ever charged, and I thought that my safest course was to say nothing and lie low.

Then, about a year ago, I was astounded to find myself face to face with Rachel Appleton when she set me up for a robbery. I said nothing, fearing that if I betrayed to the police how I had guessed who she was, my connexion with Len Appleton would be investigated again. I preferred to do a couple of months' time for burglary than be arrested for murder. When my house was broken into while I was doing time -- the new pane of glass was a give-away - but nothing was taken, I realised that she had struck again, probably to possess herself of my keys. I also guessed she might try the same trick again. Then one day, when I accidentally caught sight of her walking purposefully into town a week after another robbery, this time at a building society, I followed her. She entered my house, as I thought she might, with incriminating evidence. I spoke to her, and she made the mistake of saying that she was going to persecute me for the rest of her life because of what I had done to her father. I determined that I was going to be free of this permanent menace. I got my pistol and shot her twice. I 'hid' the evidence as you know, thinking to persuade the police, as I succeeded in doing, that I had been set up again. The rest is probably known, as Inspector Wickfield's investigation was thorough and intelligent. How he got on to me I do not know, but I admire his perseverance and congratulate him and extend my humble thanks.

Trudy says I should have approached the police and confessed much earlier, but I held out, hoping to escape detection. I realise now that the effect of this was to put an intolerable strain on Rachel's family and her husband, and I regret it. I am consoled by two thoughts. The first is that my wife has been an inestimable support, for which I can never thank her enough, particularly after the way I treated her for many years of our marriage. The second is that I can atone for my crimes and so prepare eventually to meet my God.

Signed this fourth day of July 1972.

Michael Napier